THE END
OF THE WORLD
AS WE KNEW IT

Books by Nick Cole

CTRL-ALT REVOLT!

The End of the World as We Knew It

The Old Man and the Wasteland (The Wasteland Saga)

The Savage Boy (The Wasteland Saga)

The Road is a River (The Wasteland Saga)

The Red King (Book One of Wyrd)

The Dark Knight (Book Two of Wyrd)

Soda Pop Soldier

THE END
OF THE WORLD
AS WE KNEW IT

NICK COLE

The End of the World as We Knew It

Nick Cole

Published by Castalia House
Kouvola, Finland
www.castaliahouse.com

Cover Design by M. S. Corley

Worlds end all the time.

Ask any sixth grader at school year's end,

Adulthood's beginning,

Worlds end as they must.

Now, all we'll have is the sound of lonely lanyards
on night's breeze to remind us of our long gone
games.

To remind us worlds end,

All the time

Contents

This piece was inspired by the events of the Plague. I call it *The End of the World as We Knew It*. It is the artist's intention that this work, three independent accounts, not be taken as a complete history regarding the events of those terrible days in which eight tenths of the world's population perished. Instead, it is hoped, by those of us who work within the kaleidoscope that is Historical Art, that this piece, these three separate accounts, will bring a greater understanding of ourselves through the lens of time.

—Kanterbury Voss, Historical Artist

Part One: Revelation

Voice Memos

The following is a transcription of voice memos recovered from a site near Corona Del Mar, California, during the Reconstruction in the months after the outbreak. The contents were located on a smartphone found inside an employee locker located in a high-end, open-air, retail mall.

Voice Memo 1

(Female Voice) I'm so hung-over. *(Car noise in background)* I have no idea what happened last night.

Again. *(Tape edit)*

It's three o'clock, it's hot, and I'm dragging. I've got to stop drinking.

But... I'm afraid.

To be truthful, like Dr. Connors and Jason want me to be... I'm afraid of what I'll do next when I'm drunk. One morning I'm going to wake up and there'll be someone dead. I don't even want to think about that right now. But maybe if I do, I'll stop. I've got to stop before the wedding. I've got to stop for Jason. I've got to stop for him.

Voice Memo 2

(Female voice, cackling laughter) You should have seen your face when the... *(More laughing)* when the... *(More laughing)* when the alarm went off and the security door *(More laughing, cackling)* slammed shut. You looked like... *(More laughing)* *(Male voice in background, unintelligible)*

Voice Memo 3

This is the worst day of my life. Worse than the first day of college. Far worse. I'm not erasing that memo from last night. I'm going to keep that as a reminder for the rest of... for the rest of my life, however long that is. And every time I listen to it, I'm gonna remember exactly what I did. Even though I really can't remember. Mostly.

I slept with Matt. Dammit! It sounds so stupid. I slept with my boss. Dammit, dammit, dammit.

I need a drink more than I've ever wanted one in my entire life. I hate Southern California. I hate my life.

(Edit)

This is gonna hurt but I'm going to admit it anyway.

I slept with Matt Hastings.

There, I said it. I told the truth. The ugly, awful, and stupid truth.

(Crying)

There's more. Just so you remember, Alex. Alexandra.

Now I sound just like my mother.

I am marrying the man I love in six weeks.

I am so sorry, Jason. I really am.

I don't know what to do. I could tell you but… you'd end it.

I would.

Damn.

None of this would've happened if yesterday hadn't been so damn scary. It's all this Black Ops crud. I should be working on a national laundry detergent campaign or a Louis Vuitton rollout. Not theorizing whether people are going to freak out regarding the Chinese Virus.

Of course they're going to freak out!

They're going to pitch a fit when they find out what happened to all those people.

Sounds convenient, Alexandra. Blaming your drinking problem on the modern equivalent of the Black Plague. Was it the Black Plague's fault in college? Did the Black Plague land you in jail twice? Jason's not gonna buy the Black Plague when you tell him about Matt.

No, he's not. And why am I having a conversation with myself?

Because Doctor Connors said you should. You should confront yourself the morning after, using these voice memos. Try to answer your own questions. That's what he would say.

So why did I sleep with Matt?

And while I'm on that subject, why am I such a screw up?

I don't know. I don't know.

(Call waiting sound)

(Edit)

Now I'm scared. Oh man...

Voice Memo 4

I'm leaving this as a record. I don't know what's going to happen... what's happening. But, I need to leave a record. My name is Alexandra Watt. I work for Gorham and Kennicker Advertising in Manhattan. For the past two weeks, I've been in Southern California working on a secret government project called Gravedigger, which is being conducted inside a lab known as the Dome located in Long Beach. Stupid secret project name, huh? Well, I'm blabbing everything I know about Gravedigger. This is my insurance.

Who am I kidding?

They're going to kill me.

Gorham and Kennicker were hired to diagnose the public relations aspect of a problem, if it becomes public knowledge that... that the U.S. Government tried to develop the super-virus that's wiping out China.

That's not fair, for the record.

China developed it first.

I need a drink.

(Edit)

Okay, I feel weirdly stable. Really stable. I'm not kidding, that was the worst I've ever needed a drink in my life.

(Sigh)

I stopped at a bar in Long Beach. Some dive called the 36/36 club. It was quiet in there. The owner, a guy named Blake, said his day manager didn't show up.

It's been really quiet all throughout Long Beach where I've been staking out the Dome across the water. Now that I really think about it, not a lot of cars out either. Zero people on the streets.

It's not the virus. I need it not to be that damned virus.

I need it so badly not to be that virus. Those emergency doors inside the Dome, that was a system fault. That's all. Just like they told us.

From the handouts the public was never supposed to see, that virus, if it's anything like its Chinese equivalent, should have killed us all by now. So, I admit my thinking's a little colored by all the black and white photos and reports I wish I'd never seen. That's all.

For the record, I was trying to find out what was going on back at the lab today. But I didn't want to get any closer than Belmont Shore. I could see the Dome on the other side of the water from there. It was swarming with helicopters. So I guess the lab was…

This is bad.

For the record, the lab was compromised.

For the record, I was in it.

The Staff, General Barnes and his aid. Me and Matt.

We were all there.

Right now I'm parked in my rental outside the 36/36 Club. Parked in front of a laundromat. There's a liquor store down the way. I'm going to get some more booze.

Hell, I'm probably dying anyway.

Voice Memo 5

Maybe this is how the virus works. I mean, I cannot get drunk enough. I just drank an entire bottle of Aftershock. I know, Aftershock, it's so Marcus from college.

I should be dead.

But I feel great.

Heck, looking in the rearview mirror... I look great, and that's not just the voice of Marcus talking. Marcus. I wonder whatever happened to you after college. Who the hell cares anymore.

For the record, I just bought a bottle of vodka, some Aftershock, and some whisky. The plan is to go back to my hotel in Corona Del Mar and drink myself silly until they finally figure out where I'm hiding and come pick me up. Then, I imagine it's two bullets in the head and one to the heart, or however it is those Black Ops dudes do it.

I'll say one thing about Matt. It was his good idea to ditch the hotel the government had us in and move south down to Newport along the coast. The government has no idea we've been staying in Corona Del Mar. For the record, in light of current events, that was a good idea.

But, that's not the record is it?

No, the record is... the record is I did it with Matt.

I have no memory of initiating it or how it took place or why I would even want to for that matter. I think I might have woken up during, and there was Fat Matt. Doing his thing.

I need a drink.

(Paper bag sounds, drinking sounds)

I'm gonna nurse this.

(Extended drinking sounds)

Quarter bottle in one go. Yikes.

Man, there is no one out today.

About Matt... I'm so sorry, Jason. I really am. I had no intention of ever doing anything like this to you. But I did, and I take full responsibility for it. I did it and I'm so sorry.

(Drinking sounds)

I guess I got carried away. I want to blame the liquor, or the fear, or how hungry I felt, but really, I'm the only one to blame. Stupid Alex again.

We went out drinking, me and Matt. After that damned false alarm at the Dome, we both just felt we needed to take the edge off. It felt like the real deal when those sirens went off. It felt as though we were going to end up like the two corpses on the floor of the quarantine room. So Matt says afterwards, "I need a drink." He doesn't know I have a problem. Your boss can't know you have a problem with drinking. It means you're weak. So I thought, "I'll just have one." I had a plan. Just one. And one leads to many. Many leads to bed. It was like I was on autopilot. Like I was hungry for booze. Hungry... for something.

Yikes.

For the record, I don't think the U.S. government was trying to make a weapon. Super Science, what a joke. Everyone wants to live forever. From what the report says, the Chinese were developing some sort of new Longevity Serum. But it got out of hand and started killing everyone instead. A place called Yulin was completely wiped out and the whole world doesn't even know a Chinese city is basically dead.

The only people who know are what's left of a SEAL Team and the twenty people inside the Dome. I doubt if the President even knows.

(Drinking Sounds)

I doubt if the President even knows. That's funny, isn't it? You'd think he'd know about everything we as a nation are up to. Not this... this is too big for a mere politician to handle.

I know it's wrong to drink and drive, but I'd better get the hell out of here. I'll talk while I drive.

(Drinking sounds)

(Car ignition)

(Street noise throughout the rest of the memo)

Tanner the Spook called me this morning. Told me to come in and get tested. CIA jerk. What was Gorham and Kennicker thinking when they took this contract with them?

I said to Tanner, "What're you saying?"

He says, "I'm saying, come in and get tested."

There's an evil man.

I asked him if that meant the lab had been compromised yesterday when the alarm went off. He tried to tell me it was a False Positive.

I knew he was lying when he asked me where I was at that moment.

I acted scared and said I'd be right in. I think he bought it. Told me not to worry. "It's just a precaution."

Seeing what I saw, hearing what I heard while staking out the Dome from Belmont Shore in our rental Mustang, showed me it wasn't a False Positive. Not by a long shot.

I swear... I heard gunfire coming from across the water.

(Drinking sounds)

Almost finished with the vodka I just bought. Yikes.

Okay, since this is a record. What's in the Dome?

The Dome was an old museum. A long time ago. Some giant plane Howard Hughes bought was stored there. I think they shot a Batman movie in it once. Matt told me that. Now it's probably ground zero for the American production of The Chinese Virus Show.

If I understand my "Eyes Only" handouts right, then I've got about twelve hours to go before I'm dead like the corpses in the quarantined Hot Zone room.

Inside the Dome is a quarantined Hot Zone room.

Inside the Hot Zone are two bodies.

Special Operator Badshelter and an unknown Chinese peasant.

As far as I can tell, they've been dead for about two weeks.

We were told they both died from the Chinese Virus, according to Professor Marks as told to General Barnes.

Except I noticed something weird about both bodies.

(Drinking Sounds)

Man, it's completely dead out.

I noticed each corpse inside the Hot Zone had some kind of wound to the back of its head. They were lying face up. But every day, the bottom of the floor they were lying on would have some... there was stuff coming out of their heads. Like they had a wound in the back of their skulls.

So what happened?

If they died of the virus why did they have an open wound in the back of their skulls?

General Barnes says the virus is breaking down the cell structure of the brain and it's "reducing" out the back of the skull, his words not mine. Out through...

But that makes no sense.

So that's everything I know.

Eleven hours and change to go.

(More drinking)

Voice Memo 6

I'm back in my room and I've been drinking for an hour. Not only should I be hammered, I should be dead. I finished the vodka after the whisky after the Aftershock. I stopped at some giant-sized liquor store and bought a cardboard box full of booze. Really top-shelf stuff, too. If I'm going to be dead in eleven hours then... who cares? If not... well, I'll be happy to be alive regardless of the charges on my card. You should've seen the doorman in the lobby when I brought in a box full of jingly-bottle liquor. His eyes were wide, then cool as a cat he says, "My kind of lady."

Yikes.

I knocked on Matt's door before I went on my scouting mission to Belmont Shore this morning. No answer. I went back and knocked again this afternoon. The Do Not Disturb sign was still on the door. I have this vague memory of having left it there when I fled last night.

(Drinking Sounds)

Mmmmm... Bourbon.

Yeah. The Do Not Disturb sign. Yikes. I'm so sorry, Jason. So very sorry.

(Drinking Sounds)

When I went back to Matt's room this afternoon, after I dropped off the bottles in my room, it was just to check on him. I knocked until some lady in the next room opened the door and asked me if I minded. I stopped. I could hear him in there. He was bumping around.

But he didn't answer.

He's got a wife. They just had a baby. He probably feels like pond scum too.

Yikes.

(Drinking sounds)

(Edit)

I just got a notification on Twitter.

Some guy named Chas347 said he needs to meet me.

I bet!

(Incoming message vibration) (Edit)

Another one. Checking.

He says he wants to talk about what happened in the Dome.

Oh man, that's… that's got Tanner written all over it.

He knows I'm not coming in.

He's looking for me now.

I know…

(Drinking sounds)

I know they're gonna whack me. Or make me disappear.

I'm not ready yet. I've got ten hours to go. Ten hours to really live it up. I want to do a few things first.

Get really drunk.

Write a letter to Jason. Explain everything.

Watch a chick flick and listen to loud music.

Call Jason.

Yeah, I should do that. I won't tell him what's going on, I'll just…

(Incoming message vibration) (Edit)

Tanner again, pretending to be Chas347. Says he's a friend. Says he's in the same boat.

Yikes.

(Drinking Sounds)

This is heart attack serious.

Voice Memo 7

I think… there are like five hours to go.

I am a drunken mess. All the booze really caught up to me a few minutes ago.

I'm almost finished with the case of… bottles everywhere. I'm looking for one to… Here it is.

(Drinking sounds)

That's the stuff.

I should be a lot worse off. Maybe drinking's doing something to slow the virus.

(Drinking sounds)

Yes.

Better.

The guy from Sal's Beachtime Video was here.

(Yelling) Hey, are you still in the bathroom?

Nope. Empty.

(Edit)

I have blood in my mouth.

Is that a symptom?

I can't remember.

The guy from the video store brought me my movie. I offered him a drink. We started watching Rosencrantz and Guildenstern are Dead… then what?

I can't remember.

I wanted to watch Rosencrantz. I didn't want a chick flick like I thought I would. I thought I wanted to watch Four Weddings and a Funeral, but then I knew I'd call you, Jason, and tell you everything and I can't do that. But I still need to call you.

I need to call you, Jason, and tell you that I really, really love you. That's important. I need to do that. I need to tell you that I blew it and that I'm drinking again.

So the guy... a kid really, who brought the movie over after work, I said I'd give him a hundred dollar tip if he did, we had a drink, I think. I checked my wallet and all my travel money's still there.

So where did he go?

I'm going to need some more booze if this party's gonna keep going. I should be dead by 3 a.m. "if" I'm infected with the virus. Big if.

Liquor stores close at two.

I should bust a move and get that liquor. It's not going to get it itself.

I know I'm a drunk. I mean, I know I have a problem. I've had one since college. No one—I mean no one—knows how bad it really is. Not my parents, not my college roommates. Not even Jason, probably. No one ever figured it out.

Maybe it even got better while I was with Jason?

I never noticed before now, but I guess it kinda did.

When I woke up a few minutes ago, my engagement ring was missing. I thought the kid from the video store had maybe stolen it while I was blacked out or unconscious. But he hadn't. I'd put it in the secret pouch inside my suitcase.

It's a beautiful ring. Not just expensive. Jason's the best broker on the Street, he can afford a lot. But it's classy too. Using the word "classy" might be a dead giveaway that I don't know what I'm talking about. But it's got style. And then there's the rock. Big, but not too big. Big enough. In certain lights, there's almost a red glimmer deep down inside of it.

If anyone would've ever told me that someday I'd get a ring like that from someone who actually loved me, I wouldn't have believed it. I still don't.

Maybe that's for the best. Leaving it in the pouch might be for the best. I need to tell Jason the truth, about everything, before I put it back on. About the drinking. About Matt. About everything.

What's left of our relationship after that, if there is anything left, might be worth something.

My drinking has been worse. I mean nothing like tonight, but since the car accident last year it had gotten a lot better. There are some vacations I took where I did nothing but drink. And I can drink a lot. But this is by far the most I've ever drank. Still, it doesn't seem to affect me much. Then all of a sudden, Whamo!

Voice Memo 8

Still no one out. I know Orange County rolls up its sidewalks at nine but still, this is the Gold Coast. This is where the Lakers' biggest star lives. You'd think there'd be some kind of late-night crowd.

Nothing. It's very quiet out there tonight.

I found a liquor store and bought three cases of booze.

That's the most booze I've ever bought at one time.

That's crazy.

Or at least, that's what the guy behind the counter must've thought.

I told him I was having a party.

He said, "Some party."

Tanner as Chas347 has been tweeting me since this afternoon.

When 2 a.m. rolls around, I'll tell him I'm at the Pacific Hotel. Then he can drive down here to Newport in the dead of night and pick me up. By three, I'll either be dead or have a clean bill of health.

That's my only hope.

Which is kinda sad. I'll either be dead, or not dead.

I'm down to the basics here.

Yikes.

Voice Memo 9

It's two o'clock in the morning. Just after. I finally tweeted Chas347 and told him where I was. Room 709. He said he was on his way.

Right, Tanner. I know it's really you.

(Drinking sounds)

Voice Memo 10

I never did set the record straight, did I?

Fifteen minutes until Tanner gets here. I should be... I don't know, rife with symptoms. What were they? Sweating, vomiting. Cramps. Bleeding. Muscle soreness. I've got none of those. On the whole, I'd have to say... I feel great. Really great.

Then again, I just drank all the booze in the world, so there's that to consider. But when I look in the mirror, I feel... I look good. Twenty-eight. Blond. Short hair, sort of French model. Muscular. I do Pilates, you know. I saw the photos of the people who'd contracted the Chinese Virus.

I don't look like a walking corpse.

Jason liked to tell me I looked like the singer from Blondie. Yeah, that band from the eighties.

Still, Tanner's probably gonna whack me. I knew it from the minute I met that guy, he's evil. You can see that in people, sometimes. He's the guy who does someone else's dirty work and doesn't mind a whole lot.

I tried Matt's room again. No answer.

So, for the record...

Jason, if you ever hear this, and I don't think you will, I'm... love you. I love you. I'm in love with you. I want to say I'm sorry for the whole Matt thing. It didn't even feel like me who was doing... that. I'm sorry for lying about my drinking. I never should have said "yes" to your proposal. At least, not until I told you how bad my drinking's been, and then went to rehab.

I didn't lie about Matt. But then again, I haven't had a chance to. So maybe I would've.

No Jason, I'm sorry for lying to you about who I really am. I may look normal, but I'm not. I'm sick, Jason. I'm not a monster, I'm just sick, that's all. I'm sorry you fell in love with a girl who looked like Blondie from the eighties. I wish I could've been someone else. You were the best thing that's ever happened to me. I should call you now, but you're probably still sleeping. Big day on Wall Street tomorrow. I bet you'll make a million dollars.

I wasn't worth it.

But you are.

You're worth a million dollars... to me.

(Drinking sounds)

Voice Memo 11

(Whispering) I'm turning this on to record my meeting with Tanner. Chas347 tweeted from the parking lot. He's on his way up. I just heard the elevator in the hall. It's after three in the morning. I know Tanner'll find my phone. But maybe somehow these memos will end up in the record. Maybe someone will know. Maybe someone with a kind heart will tell Jason I loved him.

Do I have too much faith in humanity?

(Drinking Sounds, light knocking)

Here I go.

(Male Voice) Are you Alex Watt?

(Female Voice) Did Tanner send you? I'm not sick. I'm still alive, see? It's been eighteen hours since whatever happened at the lab happened. I'm good.

(Male Voice) I don't know any Tanner, lady.

(Female Voice) Are you going to kill me?

(Male Voice) Can we talk inside the room?

(Movement sounds)

(Drinking sounds)

(Female Voice) (Whispering) For the record, Chas347 is a good-looking giant black dude. *(Full voice)* Drink Chas, or do I call you Mr. 347?

(Male voice) Are these all... did you drink all these by yourself, lady?

(Female Voice) Well, there was a guy here from the video store, I think he had a drink.

(Male Voice) You have a problem.

(Female Voice) Hmm... I'll have to look into that.

(Drinking sounds)

(Female Voice) So if you're not Tanner, and Tanner didn't send you, then who are you and what do you want?

(Male Voice) My name is Les McMath. Lester McMath the Third. Lt. Commander, U.S. Navy.

(Female Voice) So you're with them?

(Male Voice) Listen, lady, I don't know what's going on. I mean, I probably know more than you. Maybe you know some of the

story that I don't. But, I'm betting you're scared. I'm betting you're not with the government. This Tanner guy, I don't know him personally, but I know the type. He's probably the shot caller for JSOC.

(Female Voice) The what?

(Male Voice) It means he's overseeing the operation, for Joint Special Operations Command.

(Female Voice) Sounds right. I mean… should I be telling you this?

(Drinking sounds)

(Male Voice) What you should do, is stop drinking.

(Female Voice) If I stop, I don't feel so hot.

(Male Voice) Have you had any of the symptoms?

(Female Voice) No, nothing like that. I'm fine. I'm just an alcoholic.

(Male Voice) You haven't had any of the signs since the last time you were at the lab?"

(Female Voice) No. I'm fine. Really. Does this mean I'll make it?

(Male Voice) I don't know. I'm just a pilot.

(Female Voice) I don't understand.

(Male Voice) I need to tell you something and I think you might be the only person I can trust right now. You and your partner Matt Hastings. Long story short, I think something big is happening. You're the only civilians involved. The rest are government. Chances are, they'd kill me if they knew I was still alive.

(Female Voice) I don't understand… were you at the Dome, Mc-Math?

(Drinking sounds)

(Male Voice) Lady, I don't know what's going on at the Dome. I mean, I have an idea, but I don't know for sure what's really happening.

(Female Voice) Then how do you know about me and Matt?

(Male Voice) I swiped the visitor log sheet from the gate. You two were listed as representatives of some civilian contractor. Gorham and Kennicker. You lawyers?

(Female Voice) No, we do marketing. So you don't know what's going on inside the Dome?

(Male Voice) I have a guess.

(Female Voice) Yeah, and what's your guess?

(Male Voice) There's a dead Chinese peasant in there.

Voice Memo 12

This is Alexandra Watt speaking. I'm making this audio recording with Lester McMath, Lt. Commander U.S. Navy, on Thursday night, no wait… Friday Morning, August 31st. It's about four thirty-five. The sun will be up soon. So there's that to look forward to. Lt. Commander, should I call you that, or just Commander?

(Male Voice) McMath will do fine. But, for the record… my name and rank is Lt. Commander Lester McMath. On the books I'm assigned to the Third Naval Air Wing out of San Diego. But

that's just for show. My real assignment is to fly a "speck" Ops C-130 for JSOC and report to Admiral Childs directly.

On the fourteenth of August, this year, I was ordered to fly a covert ops mission into Mainland China and drop a SEAL Team near Yulin, north of the border with Vietnam. Two nights later, flying nap-of-the-earth, I landed my bird in a field just west of the city. The SEAL Team boarded with one passenger. Or, should I say, what was left of the SEAL Team. Only eight members of the twenty-nine man team made it back to the bird.

For the duration of the flight, the deck, the flight deck that is, was off limits to the team and vice versa. Only Chief Jones had contact with the SEALs.

We were told to head out to sea off the Chinese Coast and bear toward the South West Coast of the United States. We refueled twice while airborne and didn't get our exact heading until much later in the flight. Eventually we were vectored in to Long Beach, California.

(Female Voice) That's when things began to get… bad, Lt. Commander… McMath, I mean?

(Male Voice) Real bad. Things got real, real bad.

We got our approach clearance into Los Alamitos, but over the outer marker we were waved off and told to head back out to sea. Clearance came from an AWACS, which was unusual. Those things only fly over strategic operations areas. Theatres of war, basically. So what one was doing over Los Angeles, I don't know. But whatever was happening, it was big. For the last few years, flying JSOC, I've gotten used to that type of thing.

I took the controls from Allen... that's Lt. Allen, my Co-Pilot, James. He was a really good man. So, I took the controls as he started getting our new heading and altitude from Command.

It was right about then we heard the gunfire, sustained and for about a minute, coming from the cargo deck in the back of the aircraft.

Allen radioed Command, telling them we had a problem in the back. We got an Admiral Solomon on the line who told us to pay no attention to what was going on in back of the aircraft and fly the course heading we'd been given.

So I flew it. What else was I supposed to do?

Then the door light indicator from the rear cargo deck went on. Someone was opening the cargo door. I called the Chief and tried to get him to tell me what was going on back there. No answer. He was a good man too.

Solomon told us to descend to fifteen hundred and fly past the Queen Mary, heading out to sea on a compass bearing of two-seven-zero. I told Allen to open the flight crew weapons locker, and executed the turn over Long Beach, heading across the bay toward the peninsula. Terminal Island, off to my right, was all lit up with cranes and tankers. Once we passed over the peninsula where the Queen Mary is docked, and that big Dome where they used to keep the Spruce Goose, I was told to climb to flight level angels one seven, heading course two-seven-zero. Due west.

I don't know what happened on the cargo deck. But fifteen hundred is Jump Altitude, and one of those SEALs must have gone out the back with the Chinese guy. After that, Command ordered us to climb to altitude over the ocean. Mission complete, I guess.

I told Allen to go in back and check the cargo deck.

A minute later, he called up front to the flight deck and told me they were all dead. Including Chief Jones. Like I said, good man. Fine man. Wife and five kids.

I don't know how much longer after that, maybe a couple of seconds, we're climbing through five-thousand, when the ground-to-air missile alarm went off in our electronics package. I yanked my bird to port and leveled out, popping flares, but the missile hit us pretty quickly.

(Long Pause)

(Female voice) What'd you do then?

(Male Voice) I ejected.

(Short Pause)

(Female Voice) Go on. You need to finish.

(Male Voice) Why don't you share some of that booze?

(Sounds, indeterminate)

(Drinking sounds, near and far)

(Male Voice) I punched out. Came to in the water, maybe a few miles offshore.

(Female voice) What did you do then?

(Male Voice) I made my way to shore. Then I spent the next week hiding out in motels. I can't imagine they think I survived. They should've had a Search and Rescue team out looking for me in the water. But I think they were trying to put this operation together on the fly. So my guess, and this is nothing but conjecture, they

didn't have any kind of SAR team on standby to look for survivors because they didn't want there to be any survivors.

(Female voice) So who do you think shot you down?

(Male voice) I don't know who pulled the trigger. Destroyer off-shore out of San Diego could've done it. Stinger team on the peninsula for sure. I don't know who pushed the button. But JSOC ordered whoever it was that did it, to do it.

(Female Voice) Why?

(Male voice) Cleaning up.

(Drinking sounds)

(Male Voice) They probably figured everybody on board... well let's put it this way, someone on board, was likely infected with whatever's going on in China. Best way to handle it was to get their operative, whoever he was, off the plane and into the water near the Dome for extraction.

(Female Voice) Special Operator Badshelter. Does that name sound familiar?

(Male voice) Never met him. Never met any of 'em. They probably got this Badshelter to secure the prisoner and jump after he took out the rest of the team and Chief Jones.

(Female voice) Why kill the team?

(Male voice) I survived in the water and made it back to shore. Every pilot gets a standard escape and evasion course, but when I started flying JSOC, I got a little more. Those SEALs on the other hand, it would've been no problem for any one of them to follow the first jumper out and make it back to shore. Even if they were wounded. Command was probably trying to make sure any

survivors on the Seal Team didn't do just that when they shot us down. Coulda' been their plan to cut down on exposure to the virus. But that's just a guess.

Historical Artist's Note

I have allowed the following Incident Investigator's notes to remain in this portion of the transcript. While adding color and depth to the overall piece, most of the historical data is common knowledge. But, in this particular account, the Investigator who compiled and archived these transcripts shortly after the Plague, during the second phase of Reconstruction, has his own story to tell. His summation, at the end of this section of the piece, of the times and events, is heartbreaking, even so far removed from those dark days.

Investigator's Note

Early reports of the outbreak may have been recorded within three days of Lt. Commander McMath's account of the shootdown. Along the coast from Terminal Island to Palos Verdes, criminal activity was suspiciously high in the last two weeks before the initial outbreak of the Plague. Police department records that survive indicate an above average incidence of bizarre behavior and violence in the days leading up to the generally accepted start date of the Plague. Though not confirmed, it would appear that some members of the SEAL team, possibly infected and assumed terminated, may have escaped after Special Operator Badshelter jumped with the test subject. These reports all exist well prior to September 1, the officially recognized start date of the Plague.

—*F. Darrow, Sr. Review Investigator, Department of Reconstruction, New California Republic.*

Voice Memo 12 resumes

(Male Voice) So they killed 'em. They killed 'em all.

(Female Voice) He. Badshelter. He killed them all. *(Pause)*

(Male Voice) They. They killed those men.

Voice Memo 13

McMath is asleep. Curled up near the window in a chair. Sun's not up yet, but it's getting light in the east. Lots of fog. It's actually really nice.

McMath wants us to take this public.

I don't see that we have much of a choice. If I wasn't sure whether Tanner would whack me or not, after McMath's story, there's little doubt that's the plan.

Our plan, on the other hand, is to buy a car with cash, or steal one. Then drive back to New York. That should take two days driving in shifts. We'll go right to a contact I have at the network. We'll give them the story.

They can't kill us then.

Plus, it's been well over the incubation period for me. I should be dead. McMath should have died a week ago. So I don't think either of us are infected. Hooray for me.

Voice Memo 14

There's smoke in the air. It's still foggy and we can't see much because we're on the 7th floor. For the week that Matt and I have been staying at the hotel, I've smelled the ocean every morning. When we first checked in, I told myself I'd go running. Not drink. I guess we know how that went.

But this morning there's smoke.

I also heard sirens, a lot of them. Police and fire a while ago. Now it's weirdly quiet.

McMath's taking a shower. He went to his car and came back with a duffel bag. I saw a gun in there.

This is getting out of hand.

Have I made the right choice? What if McMath is just some lunatic? What if this is all a psychotic break, or a delusion brought on by my binge? I've been drinking so much…

(Drinking sounds)

Better.

I've been drinking so much, maybe this is just a psychotic episode.

Voice Memo 15

Oh man. Okay.

(Drinking Sounds)

The plan is gone.

(Background noise. Possible helicopter, police variant type)

As soon as McMath got out of the shower, I went to take one last look at the parking lot. There's a ritzy open air mall across the street. Usually the employees are parking at the edge of the parking lot and walking into the mall about this time of the morning. Not today.

There are two squad cars out there. Police cars. When I stepped out onto the balcony, one of the deputies touched the mic on his vest and spoke. They were looking directly at me.

Ten minutes ago, two helicopters showed up.

It was Tanner.

He called me and Matt by name over a loudspeaker and told us to come out of the hotel with our hands up.

There are snipers hanging off the sides of the other chopper.

Voice Memo 16

There's a crowd of people forming in the parking lot.

I don't know what to do...

(Background Noise: Helicopter. Someone in the room talking. Possibly Lt. Cdr McMath)

Voice Memo 17

Jason, this message is for you.

(Background noise: small arms fire. Male voice yelling, wood splintering)

(Male Voice) Get it together lady! Drop that bottle and get to the elevator!

(Background noise, indeterminate)

(Female voice) The snipers are shooting at us!

Jason... *(Heavy breathing, drinking sounds)* The snipers are shooting at us.

We're in the hallway. We... *(Heavy breathing)* left the room to get away from the snipers. One almost shot McMath. But that's not the worst... *(Drinking sounds, small arms fire)* Something happened to Matt.

I ran to his door... *(Soft bell sounds, possibly the elevator)* It was off its hinges. Matt was on... his door was smashed, but he was stuck on the other side of it. It was blocking him from leaving the room. His arms were all bloody. He was still naked. His eyes... he was gray, Jason, like he was dead. He... growled at me.

(Crying)

(Background noise soft bell. Elevator door opening)

(Female Screaming)

Voice Memo 18

We're in the stairwell now. McMath is trying to break open the door to the suite on the top floor of the hotel. A man with wild eyes came out of the elevator and grabbed me. McMath pushed him off me and threw the man back inside the elevator. This is crazy!

(Sounds. Loud metallic clanging. Grunting)

Jason I want to tell you everything. I want to tell you how sorry I am that I lied to you about who I truly am. I'm so sorry. I wanted to be the person you thought you could love.

(Drinking sounds)

Wait!

(Smashed glass)

Damn. I dropped the only bottle I managed to get out of the room.

Well... I guess I'll have to quit drinking.

For now.

Voice Memo 19

I broke open the liquor cabinet in the suite. So, game on. Which is good, because in the five minutes I went without a bottle, at least taking small sips, I began to feel awful. I felt dead inside, emotionless, but at the same time I felt every nerve in my body, and they were all on edge. I felt really angry.

If I don't drink myself to death, I'm going to need to be hospitalized.

Those helicopters are still circling outside the hotel. They're trying to find us.

Matt was crazy. He must be infected with the virus. He looked like hell. The guy in the elevator too.

But why am I not sick?

We were both in the lab. If he was exposed, so was I.

We had... sex. So...

(Male voice) Alex, check this out! The police are shooting at people.

(Distant popping sound)

(Sound of woman's heels on marble)

(Female voice) They're not falling down.

(More popping sounds)

(Male voice) Don't look.

(Loud ripping sound. Possible helicopter-mounted mini-guns. Also identified heavy caliber rifle fire sounds)

(Male voice) The helicopters are using their chain guns to try and stop them!

(Female voice) For the record, whoever finds this smartphone, this is seriously out of control now. The crowd that was watching the police attempt to take us out, attacked the sheriff's deputies in their squad cars. The deputies fired back, but the crowd... kept coming.

(Drinking sounds)

(Male voice) They're still coming. Those mini-guns aren't doing anything to them!

(Female voice) Is that possible? They're just dragging themselves forward.

That one just... no!

(Drinking sounds)

He's... the deputy...

(Drinking sounds)

(Male voice) We've got our own problems. The other chopper just set down on the roof. They're probably coming in to get us.

Voice Memo 20

This is Alex still letting whoever finds my phone know what's going on. If you find me dead, blame Tanner from the project. He's the one who killed me.

I'm still hoping to make it out of here alive.

I'm still hoping to make it back to you, Jason. If I tell you the truth, and you're cool with it, we can start over again. I'll never drink. I promise. Please just let me get out of this.

Tanner called a moment ago.

He's sending the two snipers in to take us out. Actually me. He doesn't know about McMath. He says he doesn't need me alive. But if I'll cooperate, he'll do everything he can.

When I asked what that meant, he didn't say. He just said he'll do everything he can.

Tanner's circling in the helicopter now. McMath says one of the snipers will probably rappel through the big window in the suite while the other comes through either the door that leads out to the elevator, or the stairwell. He can't cover both.

He says they'll use a "flash-bang", whatever that is.

I'm hiding in the bathroom.

Voice Memo 21

It's starting. I'm recording just in case they kill me. At least there'll be a record.

I really love you Jason. I know I keep saying...

(Sound of breaking glass)

It's starting...

(A muffled whump)

(Door splintering)

(Small arms fire)

(Sound of metal rending)

(Sustained continuous small arms fire)

(Groan. Unverified but reminiscent of Plague subject vocal pattern, post-infection)

(Helicopter sounds growing louder)

(Three rapid bursts from an automatic weapon)

(Helicopter noise interrupted. Sudden increase in turbine speed and pitch deflection of helicopter)

(More automatic gunfire)

(Silence)

(Distant impact sound)

(Female Voice) McMath?

(Male Voice) Stay where you're at, girl. Don't come out here.

(Female voice) McMath…

(Male Voice) Stay. Don't even think about coming out here, lady. Just stay… I…

(Female Voice, whispering) McMath's alive, but he doesn't want me to come out yet.

(Automatic gunfire)

(Silence)

McMath? What's going on?

(Male Voice) Alright. Come out, but don't ask me what's under the sheet.

(Female voice) I won't. What happened?

(Walking sounds. Woman's heels on marble)

What happened?

(Male Voice) They came in like I said they would. I popped the one rappelling through the window. The other came through the main door. He had me. Then... well, then your friend Matt showed up from down below. Tore the door off the hinges and went straight for the one that came through the door. Sniper must have shot him with his sidearm twelve times dead center. Couldn't use the MP5, he had it trained on me. Slick as a snake that sniper pulls his side arm with the other hand and puts twelve into your friend.

Then your friend tore out the sniper's throat.

I grabbed the MP5 off the sniper dangling in the window and fired at the helicopter. I think I hit the pilot. They went down inside the mall. I finished off your friend next. I put a sheet over the two of them before you came out. Don't look, it's pretty awful.

(Female Voice) I won't.

Voice Memo 22

I drank all the booze in the mini bar. I really don't feel so good. In fact, I feel... pretty awful.

There were a bunch of sirens and cop cars making a big racket a few minutes ago. We thought they were on their way here to rescue us, but they passed by, heading North on Pacific Coast Highway. Once they were gone, it got real quiet. The sky is orange and there's thick gray smoke everywhere.

McMath says that...

I need a drink.

And I don't have one.

Still, I need one. Badly. There's got to be a ton of booze somewhere in this hotel.

Anyway, McMath says the virus seems to be getting out of control. Maybe it's just local. Maybe they're cordoning off the area. He says if we can get outside the cordon, we'll be safe.

I wanted to rip his eyeballs out when he said "safe". I'm feeling unreasonably angry and I blame it on the lack of booze.

Voice Memo 23

I need to talk to you Jason, but cell service is down. Still, I need to talk to you. Just leaving these voice memos... I feel like I am talking to you now. Even though it's not real, it helps.

My skin is crawling. If the DTs haven't started yet, and this is just a taste of what's to come, then I'm in really big trouble.

McMath says we're going to hold out here at the top of the hotel. There's only the stairwell and the elevator, and he's got that stuck on our floor somehow. Now he's busy with the stairwell door.

Outside, there're more sick people. Sick people that look like Matt. Or like Matt used to before... They're just wandering around down there. Sometimes they vomit or fall down. But they're not doing much more than that.

It's too quiet out. And it doesn't feel good.

Voice Memo 24

(Male Voice) Get inside the elevator!

(Automatic weapons fire)

Now! move it!

(Female Voice) The sick people are coming through the stairwell door, Jason!

(Female Screaming)

(Male Voice) Get the hell off...

(Automatic gunfire)

(Movement sounds. Running. A woman's heels on marble)

(More gunfire echoing off an enclosed space)

(Male voice) Stand back!

(Sound of elevator doors closing)

(Female voice) Those people... why are they attacking us?

(Male Voice) (Sighs) I don't know.

(Sounds: Magazines being ejected and inserted into various weapons)

I don't know, and we don't have many rounds left.

(Female voice) Where are we going to hide?

(Male Voice) We'll make a run for the mall across the street, out the back entrance of the hotel. Try and find someplace to hide. Maybe a bank. Those things just ripped my barricade to shreds.

Investigator's Note

This is yet another personal account that deviates from the norm of documented infected behavior. Most infected possessed little strength. It was their numbers that seemed to increase their lethality. But, in Southern California, several eyewitness accounts indicate infected that were abnormally strong, or even incredibly fast with seemingly endless endurance. The general level of ferociousness in these accounts seems much higher than the norm.

—F. Darrow, Sr. Review Investigator, Department of
Reconstruction, New California Republic.

Voice Memo 24 resumes

(Female Voice) How?

(Male Voice) Again, I don't know.

(Elevator bell)

(Female voice, screaming)

(Male voice) Hang onto my shirt and stay real close.

(Hostile groans from multiple sources)

(Automatic pistol shot)

(Three successive automatic pistol shots)

(Hostile groaning)

(Woman's heels on marble)

(Two automatic pistol shots)

(Male Voice) In there.

(Sound of heavy door being slammed)

Gimme a hand with this.

(Scraping sounds)

This should take us to the loading dock. Maybe there's a delivery truck and we can drive ourselves on outta here. C'mon.

(Female Voice) Why can't we go that way?

(Male Voice) Did you see the lobby, lady? It is swarming with those things. Are you still drunk?

(Female voice crying)

Voice Memo 25

Jason, it doesn't look good. We found a truck. But McMath can't get it started. He's got the hood up and he's trying to see what's wrong with the engine. The sick people are coming down the delivery ramp. Jason, it doesn't look like there's a way out of this.

Maybe this is for the best. Maybe I deserve this. I feel like... I feel so useless and angry. I feel... jagged, Jason. Jagged.

They're getting closer and I don't know what we're gonna do, but before they get me... I just want to...

(Male Voice, Inaudible)

(Female voice) Trying it again!

(Male Voice, Inaudible)

(Female Voice) I am turning the key! It's not...

(Engine-starting sounds)

(Squeak, then door slamming sound)

(Male Voice) Alright girl, take it nice and slow up the ramp.

(Female Voice) They're not getting out of the way!

(Male Voice) That's okay. Don't look, just keep going. Don't look!

(Loud thumps, muffled groans, cracking glass)

Easy does it, girl.

Okay, we're clear. Stop at the intersection.

(Female Voice) Hey, a plane!

(Male Voice) Where?

(Female Voice) Look. Up there. It's circling.

(Male Voice) Hold on a sec…

GUN IT NOW, NOW, NOW!

(Engine rising to max RPMs, tires squealing)

(Female Voice) They could be trying to help us!

(Male Voice) Watch out for those three in the road! That's a Specter gunship up there, it doesn't help anybody, lady. It kills people in adult-sized doses.

(Brief unintelligible groan, indeterminate sound)

(Male Voice) Right! Right! Right!

(Female Voice, Screaming) They're firing at us!

(Sounds consistent with the 30mm Chain gun carried on Specter Gunship period aircraft of this type. Multiple artillery shell impacts)

(Male Voice) Floor it! Straight into the mall!

(Explosion)

(Explosion)

(Chain gun)

Voice Memo 26

Jason, we're inside the mall now. I mean, it's not a regular mall. The stores are all out in the open. But there's a maintenance hallway that runs through the buildings. I drove the van into a fountain and we ran to the nearest store, a men's clothing store, and found the fire exit in back. We barricaded it, but it's not going to hold for long.

McMath is clearing the area now.

Once those things come for us, we won't be safe in here. We're running out of places to hide.

I think I'm sick, Jason.

I think somehow the booze has been keeping the virus… at bay, or dormant. Now that I haven't had any, I feel rotten. But that's not the worst part.

The worst part is that I want to…

I can't even say it.

I want to eat him. McMath.

It's just this… it's not like a voice. It's like a craving.

Even now, I can hear McMath banging around down the hall and I just want to run down there and rip him open.

That's disgusting.

I'm ashamed of myself.

I'm going to hide my phone. I have no idea if you'll ever find it. But, maybe… maybe this isn't as big as it seems to me.

I hope whatever is happening is only happening to me. That plane flew around shooting at everybody for a long time. Maybe the virus is just in this area and they're trying to keep it contained by killing everyone. Maybe.

File that under sentences you never thought you'd hear yourself say.

But I hope it's just here. It's bad Jason. It's really bad.

I mean, and if you knew me, knew the real me, you'd know I'm not the selfless type. But whatever it is that's made these people sick, I hope it never happens to anyone else. I hope it's just me, Jason.

I'm going to check something out and when I come back... I'm going to leave you one last message. Then I'll hide my phone.

Historical Artist's Note

This brief medical report summary was attached to the end of the transcript file in hardcopy. In reviewing the piece, I felt its inclusion at this point helps paint the narrative.

Medical File Review 11/10/47

Rumors abounded during the Plague that drinking large amounts of alcohol could indeed stave off the infection. There is no scientific evidence to support this hypothesis. Interestingly, and at this point merely conjecture, as these events and any possible lab data or samples have long since been consigned to the rubbish bin of history, it would seem that if the U.S. Military were attempting to create a retro-virus for the dead to turn on themselves, then perhaps the serotonin levels in the brain were part of the research method pursued. If this line of inquiry and the transcripts are to be believed, then yes, serotonin would have been the answer to affecting control of infected persons. Alcohol's effect on the serotonin levels in the brain would have definitely affected both the metabolic nature of what we know about the disease and the rapidity of degeneration into long-term post-infection existence. This is the only recorded evidence indicating that this may have been the case as a result of these "Black Ops" experiments at the Dome.

On a personal note: As a bit of a collector of arcane conspiracy theories from the time of the Plague, this has all the earmarks of a classic "Tall Tale". Conveniently, the West Coast Crisis Management Headquarters, the Dome, assists the tale with its spectacular demise, thus eliminating any independent verification. Also, the mysterious AC-130 gunship appears to obliterate the infected area. Obviously, a military asset of this nature used on Day One of the Plague indicates "Dark Forces" at work and fits the conspiracy narrative conveniently. In truth, it's one of my favorites. Alas, it is hardly credible.

—Ronaldo Kinglsey, MD, Chief Epidemiologist,
Department of Defense.

Voice Memo 27

(Drinking sounds)

Oh yeah…

(Drinking sounds)

Much, much better now.

Jason, I feel like everything was crazy a few minutes ago. Now, I feel right as rain. Top of the world, ma!

(Drinking sounds)

There's a bar in one of the restaurants. I grabbed four bottles and came back.

They won't last long and things look pretty bad, Jason. I don't know. I don't see a way out of this. One of those things, a sick person, is already banging on the fire door at the far end of the maintenance hall. We blocked the door with some trash carts and cardboard boxes. But even I know that's not gonna hold for long.

(Drinking sounds)

I just don't see a way out.

(Male Voice) Where the hell did you find more liquor?

(Female Voice) Restaurant bar, through there. *(Drinking sounds)* Don't worry, I was quiet. I don't think any of them saw me. Also, they're all over at the fountain, by the way. It's like a really tired rave out there. Like, the worst rave in the history of raves.

(Male Voice) You have a problem, lady. A serious problem.

(Female Voice) Well if it helps, I'll go to a meeting once we get out of here.

(Male Voice) Makin' jokes. Fine. Your buddy Tanner's helicopter crashed in the courtyard on the far side of this building.

(Female Voice) Can you fly it?

(Male Voice) I said 'crashed.' And no, even if it weren't crumpled like a beer can, I don't have a rotary wing rating.

(Female Voice) Huh?

(Male Voice) I don't know how to fly helicopters. Sounds like more of 'em at the door now.

(Drinking sounds)

(Female Voice) So what's the plan?

(Male Voice) Plan? There ain't no plan, lady. There never has been a plan. All through Annapolis all they did was drum it into us to make a plan. But how do you make a plan for what's happening out there? I'm outta options. We're outta options.

(Female voice) There's probably more guns in the chopper. We could get 'em. Maybe if we just hold out until help comes… I mean, someone has to show up eventually.

(Male Voice) All right.

Voice Memo 28

(Audible throughout recording: hammering sounds in distant background)

Jason. I'm going to finish this now. There probably isn't much time left, so this is it.

McMath is down. He's infected now. He's delirious.

Long story short, we went out through the bookstore and down to the lower level of the mall and out into a courtyard. The helicopter had come down right through the palm trees and crashed into the middle of everything.

Tanner was still inside. Trapped, mangled. Bleeding. But alive.

Those things… the sick people, they'd tried to get to him but he'd shot them in the head.

He was out of ammo and he couldn't reach the sniper rifles in back. But those things couldn't get to him. They were crawling all over the wreckage, hissing at him.

McMath shot them. Most were already torn in half or shot to pieces from the plane. But they kept crawling around, trying to get at Tanner.

While McMath got the weapons, I talked with Tanner.

I asked him why.

Why me?

He said I was infected. Like these people. Even worse though.

McMath couldn't hear him. He was busy prying off a piece of the cargo hatch.

I asked Tanner what "worse" meant. Worse means, "This has been going on in isolated incidents." His words not mine. "The global outbreak has started." Matt and I were an attempt to make a retrovirus that could infiltrate the sick and start killing them.

Except, not a retro-virus inside our bodies. Us. We were the retro-virus.

The plan was to turn us, and a significant portion of the population, against the other sick people. To make us like them, only stronger, faster, and more aggressive. They'd hoped we'd be able to retain some cognitive skills and still attack other sick people. The new fear, according to computer models they'd run, was that our infection would mutate once it mixed with theirs. All the sick people might become like us. Tanner said he'd come to clean up and make sure that didn't happen. It was nothing personal. They just didn't need to add that into the messy equation they were already dealing with.

(Audible rending sound)

They're in the maintenance hall now. It's just a matter of time before they find us in the employee locker room at the back of the restaurant.

I'm not drinking anymore, Jason.

I'm not gonna drink anymore. Ever again.

I know you knew.

You had to.

I know that you knew, because you loved me. I know that you knew and said nothing… because you love me. I know that.

(Crying)

I'm not gonna drink anymore, baby.

For you.

And for me.

McMath is almost one of them now.

It hit him quick.

We were coming back through the bookstore when one of the sick people… it was missing its legs, and it must have crawled in there after the plane shot everybody, it grabbed his leg and bit him on the thigh. Bad. He shot it.

He said…

He said…

He said, "It bit me." Then, "Damn thing bit me."

He kept it together, though. Got us back to the storage room. Barricaded it. I think, even though he didn't hear what Tanner said, I think he knew what was going to happen to him next. He kept telling me what to do after he'd done what he needed to do. He told me to get up into the air ducts. Get up on the roof. Signal for help.

He was making a plan for me.

I think he'd made a plan for himself too.

But then he just fell over and started shaking in a cold sweat. He was mumbling. Curled up in a ball.

Maybe twenty minutes after the thing bit him.

That fast.

I probably should kill McMath. Then myself. But that's murder…

Our wedding day was going to be the happiest day of my life, Jason. I just know it would've been. Like that Blondie song. Only it wouldn't have been dreaming. It would've been real.

(Sobbing)

Thank you for asking me to marry you.

You deserved so much, so much better than me.

I know you'll never stop loving… me. I know you'll come find me if you can. When you do… when you find my body, I'll have my ring on. I'm so proud… *(crying)*

I'm sober now, Jason.

That was my plan. Be sober by our wedding.

Thank you.

I'm hiding this recording, and then I'm going back to the hotel for my ring.

I took it off after Matt because I was so disgusted with myself for what I'd done. I'd been feeling that way, felt that way, every time I drank too much. Dumb stuff happened, Jason. A lot of dumb stuff. I blamed the booze and since you proposed, I've felt like taking that ring off every day because I wasn't worthy of the man who gave it to me. But I kept it on, because I wanted to be.

I wanted to be the person you thought you were marrying.

So I kept it on and I kept trying.

I thought… I thought your love could change me into something good. The someone you thought I was. The person I wanted to be.

I don't know how I'll get back to my hotel room with all those things out there.

I guess I could try the roof and then get down and run for the hotel.

It sounds like there are a lot of them outside.

It sounds like everyone in the whole world is sick and they're banging on the fire door at the end of the hall.

If I become one of them, Jason… I still love you.

I'm sober now. And I'm going to stay sober for as long as I live.

I still love you.

Even if I… become like… them, I won't be one of them, Jason. I'll be different. I'll be sober and I'll have your ring on, and maybe… I'll get better. But, I'm going to stay sober, baby.

I love you forever. I'm dreaming, Jason. Just like the song.

Thank you… *(crying)* for wanting to spend your life with me.

Incident Investigator's Notes

These recordings were found in an employee locker in the backroom of the INDUSTRIAL DESIGN BISTRO AND BAR, on a smartphone catalogued by Reconstruction in June of the next year. The Newport Beach and Corona Del Mar area, as with most of Southern California, was reclaimed within two months of the Pandemic. Unlike most of the Midwest and South, the Pandemic, though initially severe, was mild in Southern California, relatively speaking, compared to other population centers. Models indicate that only eighty-six percent of the population of Southern California was infected.

As of this date, I have attempted to determine the disposition of the persons identified in the transcripts.

Alexandra Watt Missing. Presumed Dead.

Lt. Commander McMath Terminated sometime in December outside a barricaded pharmacy in Riverside County, CA that held out through most of the Pandemic. Exact date and time of termination unclear, as survivors within the Pharmacy eventually succumbed to their attackers. ID'd corpse pile at front barricade. Shotgun wound to head. Abrasions and wounds consistent with Long-Term Post-Infection. Partial Maryland Drivers License used as ID. File Z51929941298SCR.

Marcus J. Tanner Terminated 10 October by Recovery and Reclamation Team, SGT J. Anderson. Disposition of Corpse: Trapped within wreckage of downed helicopter, Corona Del Mar. Abrasions and wounds consistent with signs of Long-Term Post-Infection.

Deputy Gil Garcia Orange County Sheriff's Department. Missing. Presumed Dead. Deputy Garcia was a First Responder to the Pacific Hotel. Police logs indicate Deputy was dispatched to aid Department of Defense Operation and provide support for one Marcus Tanner. Deputies Garcia and Wassermen were dispatched to assist from the parking lot. As indicated in the audio transcript, both Deputies were overrun. Deputy Garcia was never found.

Deputy Thomas Wassermen Orange County Sheriff's Department. Terminated, Los Angeles, Battle of City Center. Burned Corpse pile 17. Abrasions and wounds consistent with Long-Term Post-Infection. FileZ891838484SCR.

Special Operator Johanes Gustav Badshelter Presumed Dead. Listed as Killed in Action three years prior to the events of the Plague. See DOD for authentication.

Matthew Warren Hastings Deceased. Body recovered top floor of the Pacific Hotel in the Viceroy Suite. Wounds and abrasions consistent with Short-Term Post-Infection.

George Wilson Yang Terminated. One of two Delta Snipers attached to "the Dome" and commanded by Marcus J. Tanner. George Yang terminated, Battle of Los Angeles. Burned Corpse Pile 203. Wounds and abrasions consistent with Long-Term Post-Infection. FileZ119802455SCR.

Raymondo Navio Huerta Deceased. One of two Delta Snipers attached to the Op commanded by Marcus J. Tanner. Recovered hanging from roof of the Pacific Hotel. Died from wounds described in transcript. Mostly likely killed by Lt. Commander McMath with a gunshot to the head.

Brigadier General Elias H. Barnes Missing. Presumed Dead. Attached to JSOC WMD Threat Analysis Team. Presumed dead as a result of events occurring at the West Coast Crisis Management Command, or "the Dome". Body never recovered.

—F. Darrow, Sr. Review Investigator, Department of Reconstruction, New California Republic.

Historical Artist's Note

Declassified documents, no longer deemed sensitive after the 75th year, have been made available by the Department of Defense. These documents reveal that Brigadier General Elias H. Barnes ordered multiple JDAMs dropped on the Dome, where he was commanding a brave, yet futile, defense against Hyper-Modified infected created within the facility, as a result of experiments taking place in the weeks prior to the general outbreak of the Plague. I leave you with one final note from the Recovery and Reclamation Investigator who oversaw this file and entered it into the historical records regarding the Plague. I think his notes echo the sentiments of many who survived.

Incident Investigator Final Analysis

I am still not hardened to the emotional nature of these individual accounts of survival during the Plague. After two years of listening to the accounts of survivors recorded on smartphones, written down in journals, or in one instance in Western Pennsylvania, written in permanent marker on the floor of an aircraft hangar, I'm having a hard time accepting that these stories are real. That they actually happened to individuals. To people. That the person pouring their heart out in the face of terror and the destruction of life as they knew it, was just an ordinary person. A person with hopes and dreams. A dream about someday marrying her Prince Charming. I can't help thinking, wondering in fact, if in those last minutes, Alexandra Watt was waiting for her "Jason" to come to the rescue. Maybe my daughter's wedding last weekend had me thinking along these lines as I prepared the report for this transcript. After my own little girl got married, she danced with me at the reception. They played "Someday my Prince will Come" and we, my daughter and I, had one last dance. Halfway through, her husband stepped in and took over. Life goes on. Even after the end of the world as we knew it.

I can't do this job anymore.

—F. Darrow, Sr. Review Investigator, Department of Reconstruction, New California Republic.

Part Two: Reconstruction

Reconstruction Team Leader's Report

This journal was recovered on 20 December, during the first year of the Plague, at Temporary Field Site 2765, AmeriCal Gas Station and Convenience Mart off Interstate 99, San Joaquin Valley, near the town of Turleyville, CA.

Jason Hamilton, a recent team member and new recruit to the Reconstruction Corps, is the supposed author of the journal, but that cannot be verified independently as of yet. Mr. Hamilton disappeared sometime during the night of 19 December, but how and why has yet to be determined. Even though this area is clear of infected, lone stragglers and groups still appear at times. Yesterday was proof of that. Whether Mr. Hamilton violated protocol and went scavenging on his own, after hours, or whether this is yet another case of AWOL is still to be determined.

On a personal note: As leader of this team, I hardly had the opportunity to get to know Mr. Hamilton. All I remember about him was my first impression: He was weak. That he was good-looking, and weak.

Like all of us, he was just another survivor. Most of us have gotten used to not asking each other what happened. Not asking how we survived. Most of us just want to forget. I want to forget those six weeks I spent inside Dodger Stadium. But, in the Department of Reconstruction, "What happened?" and "How did you survive?" are the job.

Maybe that's the problem.

Maybe we need to start talking about what happened to us personally. I recently read that AWOLs have been rising amongst the Reconstruction Teams. Hopefully, whoever reads this report will understand that we need a new approach to what we're doing out here. Otherwise, the story of Mr. Hamilton's disappearance is doomed to be repeated ad infinitum, ad nauseum.

I do not intend to read his journal, and nothing in the regulations says I have to, unless it's assigned to me as a case for Reconstruction. I do not want to know Jason's story. I wish he didn't have one. I wish we all didn't have a story.

—Karen Haines, Reconstruction Team Leader 43

Journal

The Heart is deceitful above all things,
And desperately wicked;
Who can know it?

—Jeremiah 17:9, written in ink on the front cover,
date unknown.

October 21st

After Everything.

I couldn't do it anymore. So I came back through the Holland Tunnel and found this blank journal in the salvage pile. It was something about the quote written on the front that made me pick it out. It's time for me to write it all down. Or at least something down. Something should be written down. About what happened.

I feel the urge to tell the whole story in one line.

I'm guessing there are a lot of people now who know that one line.

I don't even know who I'm writing this journal, this message in a bottle, this signal flare, to. But I need to start talking to someone, and since I've met some people who haven't said a word since they were rescued, which I'm afraid of doing, not saying a word ever again, then I'll just talk to you.

Whoever you are.

Signal flares are used by the survivors of horrible tragedies. Airplane crashes. Rescues at sea. Lost in the wilderness.

This is my signal flare.

Whoever you are, you have a lot in common with me. You may not have been a stockbroker like me. You may not have had a privileged life of prep schools, rowing, and the Upper East Side. But whoever you are, you lived through the Plague. You are like me. We have that one tragedy in common.

So I don't need to tell you everything in one sentence.

I'm guessing you lived that sentence. Or at least I'm hoping so. Maybe that's the common ground we survivors have.

We've lived that one sentence.

Before my sudden need to tell you everything in the space of one line, I was working on the corpse clearing teams over in New Jersey, outside the Holland Tunnel entrance. I've been on the teams for the two weeks since being rescued off the top of the building I once worked in. Since being rescued, it's been two weeks of burning corpses. Two weeks of digging out the already dead.

Finding one that still moves.

Calling in the burn team.

They come over in their hazmat suits to hit it with the flamethrower.

After two weeks of digging out corpses, I've pretty much seen everything one thinks, or imagines, they will ever see in life. As an example, I give you the other night. I was sitting near the campfire outside my dorm tent, with the silent old man whose name I don't know and the Latina who doesn't speak any English. I was thinking about one of them, one of the corpses. We found it underneath a bus the army tanks had shot to pieces weeks ago, back when the corpses tried to rush the Holland Tunnel just as we were getting rescued off the rooftops. When the line between the living and the dead was very thin. Just a few soldiers thin, holding a line on a map they were told could not be broken.

It, the corpse under the bus, was still moving. Its feet were gone but that didn't stop it from going after the rats that had come down after the other dead bodies.

I sat by the fire the other night, thinking. I thought I was thinking about the thing crawling through the dirt toward us with a dead rat between its teeth. As I look back now, I wasn't thinking about that at all. I was thinking about me. About how I didn't flinch as I watched it crawl through the dust toward me. I was amazed at how I just whispered "Get a Burn Team" to the crew leader, then stood back, leaning on my shovel.

I was grateful for the break from digging. It was hot.

That's what I was thinking.

So I figured, that night around the campfire, I'd pretty much seen everything. There wasn't going to be anything that would ever phase me again. I thought this while eating my beans and rice and the tortillas we'd just started getting. Our nightly dinner. I think the Army has better rations but they stay behind their quarantine barriers in their hazmat suits.

At that moment I thought I was hardened. Untouchable.

Today we got in under the collapsed overpass that stretches the length of the kill-zone. Most of the infected had "freight-trained" down the main highway and the engineers had blown the overpass with a lot of them underneath. We expected to find a lot of movers. When we do, well, there's this running joke. It's called, "Whatever happened to Bob."

Which goes like this…

We find a male corpse that's still kicking. We're usually tired from all the digging.

"Whatever happened to Bob?" someone asks as we back away to wait for the burn team.

"Oh Bob!" someone else answers. "He went nuts. Tried to kill his whole family. I think I saw him outside a liquor store the other night trying to bash his way in."

"Good old Bob, he always loved a cold forty ounce."

Funny stuff.

Not really.

We tunneled into the side of the overpass. There were bodies buried in the dirt. Once we had a dark hole into the collapsed overpass, the crew leader shined a flashlight in and mumbled, "Live one."

A woman in a dark skirt. Torn nylons, red hair. One leg missing.

When she waved her arms at us, gnashing her teeth and making that horrible drowning-in-fluid gutter growl, I noticed she had only one hand now. The purple necrotic skin did a lot to make her look much different from the last time I'd seen her. But I should have known her by the red hair, arterial bleeding red, now dusty and wild. It had been four weeks since I had seen that hair.

After the initial outbreak, I'd survived for six weeks in the building where my brokerage used to be. I don't know how many people worked in that sixty-five story building, but there were eighty in our brokerage on the day everything went to hell in a handbasket. We had our own floor. After a few days there were only four of us left.

The thing under the overpass crawled toward us, its black teeth encrusted with gore.

I knew she'd done some modeling to pay for school before becoming a broker.

The crew leader called for the burn team and told me to step back.

I had seen that red hair in lower Manhattan four weeks ago.

I could hear the burn team pumping kerosene into their flamethrower.

For three weeks Derek from IT, Carmichael my best friend, and Kathy Henderson-Keil had survived in the Tower, once our place of work. Survived the lunatic corpse people that crawled up through the floors and stairwells after us day and night, chasing as we climbed toward the roof.

I heard someone start the igniter as the burn team pumped ripe kerosene all over her. Someone pulled me back.

Derek got it on thirty-one. Carmichael on forty-two. Kathy on forty-eight.

"Burn her!" someone screamed. She was crawling toward us fast. Even with one leg.

Kathy Henderson-Keil got it on forty-eight. That was back in lower Manhattan.

Back in another life.

The igniter caught and moments later a stream of burning fuel covered Kathy Henderson-Keil.

I'd wondered what she'd been up to since the corpses pulled her through the wall of the copy room we'd barricaded ourselves in.

Back on that day, on forty-eight, she'd disappeared into a forest of scabby gray arms and hungry roars tearing through drywall. Pulled right out of my arms.

I'd wondered what happened to her.

Her and many others.

Well, here she was.

Long time no see.

Someone laughed because she'd rolled over on her back and as she burned, her remaining leg bicycled.

"She's riding a bike!" someone laughed.

I was done digging out bodies.

I was done with everything.

I walked away with the crew leader telling me to get back to work. At the tunnel entrance, the emergency lights flickered to life. A klaxon sounded as an amplified soldier-voice told me to halt. He reminded me I would be shot.

I kept walking.

I think I wanted to be shot.

After eight weeks of hell, I was done.

I entered the tunnel while yellow safety lights bounced and strobed off bullet-riddled walls. I descended into a crater where a tank round had dug out a piece of the roadway. They were screaming at me to halt over the loudspeakers.

Just shoot me, I kept thinking. Just go ahead and shoot me.

There are snipers in the tunnel. We see them when we leave the digger camps in the morning. They have huge rifles. They wear breathing masks that obscure their faces.

One of the diggers could get bit and make it into the Safe-Zone. Then the whole thing would start all over again. The one place we've got to retreat to, Manhattan, would be gone. So there are snipers in the tunnel. They don't take chances.

I saw him ahead, sitting on a chair. His rifle rested on its tripod, on a folding card table.

I kept walking.

Just shoot me.

But he didn't.

He set the butt of the gun down. He straightened up and

looked at me from the other side of the mask. When I got to him, I just stood there looking at him.

Was he going to let me go on?

He took off his mask. He was a big man. A soldier.

He unfolded another chair and put it down next to him.

I sat down.

I began to cry.

Oct 22nd

I went for a walk today since I'm not digging out corpses anymore. Everyone in the camp stayed away from me this morning before they left for the tunnel. I walked into the city, or what remains of it. There are some streets I can't go down because they're blocked off. After a few hours, I made it to the building where my condo was. I haven't seen it since the day I left for work back in August. The street it's on has been deemed unsafe because of all the damage.

But there was no one in sight, so I slipped under the yellow tape that blocked 1st Avenue and continued on toward my building.

I knew what was coming. I had seen enough evidence on Lexington and even Park. Few buildings seemed untouched. The rest looked very much touched. The buildings that got off easy merely looked hollow. Like their eyes had been gouged out. Broken windows and unknown dark rooms lay beyond those gaping holes. At one building, I saw a corpse impaled on a flagpole that jutted out three quarters of the way down the building. No one had bothered to remove it.

The rest of the buildings were little more than skeletons. Explosions and fires had gutted them, leaving just the bones. Inside some, you'd see living rooms and barricades, kitchens and doors torn from their hinges. Shredded mattresses piled against doors where corpses had chewed their way through to get at whoever was on the other side.

There was paper everywhere. On the streets. Floating down from the sky. Everywhere.

I stood in front of what was left of my building. Someone, one of my neighbors most likely, had put up a fight. Someone had started a fire. My building had gotten the worst of the fight. Yellow tape had been wrapped loosely across the entrance. Thirty floors of blackened exposed steel climbed toward the sky.

I turned around and walked back to camp.

I guess sometimes you can't go home.

Those weeks in the Tower I'd held onto a hope. A hope that at the end of this, something would be left. My family out on the cape. Alex, safe and sound. But in reality, they had no chance. I knew what it took to survive, and I didn't see them doing that. My fiancée. She was out on the West Coast when it happened. After cell service went dead, I'd hoped she'd make it. That what was going on here wasn't the case there. She was in a hotel when things first started to get weird.

I hope she made it.

But I guess, in the end, after the fires and the dark nights, and those corpses never stopping... all you could do was run, so how could she have made it?

When did I know she didn't make it?

Except that I don't know, for sure.

After I was rescued, I figured I'd keep working until they cleared the city, and then I'd go back to my condo and start putting things back together.

I imagined picking stuff up off the floor.

That was the extent of my cleaning-up-the-apocalypse fantasy. "Oh, I guess they knocked over the speakers. Well, here they go. Right as rain."

Standing in front of my fire-gutted building, I was acutely aware that I had lived in a fantasy world for much of my life.

In short, there was nothing left. If possible, I feel even worse than yesterday. Yesterday I felt angry, humiliated, and lost. Today, I feel nothing.

Feeling nothing is worse than feeling anything else.

I returned to camp early. The Latina was making our dorm tent's usual dinner of rice and beans. I sat down in front of the fire pit and stared into the glowing ashes.

"A man," she began haltingly. I looked at her. I'd never heard her speak. "A man... from the Army... he came here looking for you today." She put her hand on my shoulder. I nodded and she turned away back to the meal.

We are all worried about each other. We are worried that the other person is not going to make it. Worried we are not going to make it as a whole, as in, "is the other person going to make it? Because I'm depending on them." Maybe it has something to do with surviving. Most people survived the Plague together, in small groups. Back on Day One, watching the streets turn into a riot of cannibals below the windows of my brokerage, I knew the whole thing was much bigger than me. But once you're in a group, you get used to worrying not about yourself so much, as worrying about the others. You worry about the guy or girl who's going to stack barricades alongside you and keep watch in the night while you're sleeping. You worry because they haven't been eating and they've been crying a lot and you need them to watch your back because you can't do everything all the time. You eventually need to get some rest. Maybe that's what all these survivors have in common. It's why they don't "off" themselves. They're making sure I'm okay. If I'm not okay, what happens to them?

They need each other.

But I'm not so convinced of that anymore.

I need to write everything down. Who I was. Who all the people I loved were. I guess in a perfect world, I'd find out what happened to all of them. At least, for the record. But that's impossible, or at this moment of societal collapse, it seems impossible. People say it will be years before we can go into certain parts of this country. I need to tell my story about the Tower.

I wonder what the man from the Army wanted from me?

I am not okay.

October 27th

I'm on a train.

The guy from the Army wanted to know if I was interested in a different job, a not corpse-digging job. Before he told me about the new job, he reminded me that if I didn't work for the community, they would have to release me from New York. I wasn't sure what that meant exactly, but I don't think anyone wants off Manhattan right now. As far as anyone knows, there really isn't any other safe place.

I said sure, as long as I didn't have to dig out any more corpses. But that was just big talk on my part. If they would have told me to dig, I probably would've gone back to digging. At least just for the free beans and rice. Seeing what was left of my building has brought my situation into perspective.

Ironically, the train is leaving Manhattan.

Irony. Taking a job to stay somewhere, but having to leave to keep the job. Irony.

But at least I have a job.

I am still, if not mentally at least physically, a member of the community.

The train will attempt to reconnect the East Coast with the West Coast. The new President feels the best way to reunite America is to show we can still connect both coasts by rail. So I'm on a heavily armored train filled with soldiers and guns.

I work in the laundry.

For the past few days, I've been folding laundry for about eight hours a day as the train slowly passes through Western New York. I think we're somewhere in Pennsylvania now, but it's pretty dark outside.

After my shift in the laundry is over, I like to stand in the breezeway between the cars and smoke. I am probably the most tired I have ever been in all my life and that includes hell week for crew, but it feels good. I did crew in college but folding laundry all day, using a steam press, is exhausting on levels never previously imagined. We drink tons of water and already my fatigues are falling off of me.

When I get to the West Coast, I'll find the hotel where Alex, my fiancée, was when it happened.

Was.

I don't want to say it. I told myself, in the Tower when it was just me, that she was dead. Everyone was dead now. I knew I was alone. But maybe there was a chance.

Wouldn't that be something to live for?

I should tell my story of the Tower. If someone is looking for me and something happens to me, this journal might give them some peace or even the closure I could use right now.

So...

I remember going to work that day on the subway. Everything seemed odd. I'd noticed things were strange, but when I thought back on it later, in the Tower when I was alone, I realized things had begun to get strange even in the days leading up to the general outbreak.

They must have been.

That morning, I'd been listening to the financial reports in my condo before going in. The regular reporter was out sick. Someone different, some guy who wasn't very experienced, was doing the report badly. As if he was distracted. He seemed more shaken than he should have been, but he got through the foreign market report. I used to go in later than most brokers. I'm... I was a specialized currency trader. Thinking back about that reporter, I believe he must have known something was up. He would've had access to the wire services. If the world was melting down and the government was doing their best to blackout the fact that huge sections of the population were, or would soon be, stark raving dead, then my guess is a lot of news reporters like him were caught in the crossfire of misinformation.

I hit the streets that morning and noticed there were less people out than usual, but I was on my Bluetooth, so I didn't pay too much attention. I remember a lot of sirens. They were roaring across town. I was annoyed. Their urgent declarations of "help on the way" were interfering with my call to a client who was intent on dumping her portfolio, and who wanted me to immediately switch gears and find her some gold.

I do... did... currency, not gold.

When I arrived at the office and got my computer fired up, the floor manager actually seemed relieved to see me. He said a lot of people weren't showing up. It was about then that Chas O'Neil came onto the floor. His hand was bleeding and he was swearing. He'd gotten into a fight with a cab driver. He'd been walking into the building, finishing a call, when the cab had coasted onto the curb. Chas had continued talking to his client, when suddenly the cabbie had lunged from the passenger door in one moment, and in the next, clamped onto Chas. Building security had raced out from the lobby and dragged the cabby off Chas, telling him to go up to his office.

"Weird day," said Carmichael. Carmichael is the only person on the floor I might call a friend.

Reading that last sentence back to myself, I realize I wrote it in the present tense. That floor, the last time I saw it, was crawling with mayhem, and as for Carmichael, he got dog-piled in the stairwell outside forty-two.

There is nothing present tense about that.

"Two guys started fighting on my train. I mean blood and everything. I got off a stop early and walked in," said Carmichael. "The heat's making people crazy." He loosened his tie. It was the dead of August. The air was drinkable. It had been blazing hot by six that morning.

"O'Neil got bitten," said the floor manager. His name was Paul Keller. He lived out on Long Island. I can't remember his wife's name.

Those last couple sentences are in perfect tense, in light of past events.

"Bitten?" asked Carmichael.

"Yeah, some crazy cab driver. It's like a full moon out or something," Paul said in his thick Long Island accent.

"Serves him right, the thief!" Kathy Henderson-Keil came through wearing that black dress and silk stockings I would see the remnants of later, underneath the collapsed overpass. Everyone, to her, was a thief.

I am the thief of her last moments.

Both of them.

The copy room and under the overpass.

That day, the first day of the outbreak, her hair is red, arterial bleeding red. It isn't dusty yet. She's a few years older than me. Pretty. Working class. Started out as an actress or a model. Got tired of being poor and got her Series Seven. She and O'Neil hated each other's guts. They were the top sellers in the office. Besides me.

That used to mean something back when there was money.

"Hey, CNN is reporting the President has declared martial law!" someone yelled across the office. I remember us standing there, looking at each other.

Whoever you are, think about that sentence.

"Hey, CNN is reporting the President has declared martial law!"

Try to remember what it was like before all this happened. Imagine yourself at home, with friends and family, at school, I don't know where. Then say those words.

What could the President have possibly declared martial law over?

That's what I was thinking.

I'm not kidding.

In the few hours that remained of what was left of civil order, I have to hand it to the government. They did a bang up job. They immediately freaked out and battened down the hatches. They told us what was up, a bit late, but at least they finally told us. It was what they told us next that got our attention. When they told us that what was happening was the most real thing that would ever happen to us, despite our ready willingness to disbelieve the incredulity of living corpses, that got our attention.

The President authorized everyone to do whatever it took to save themselves.

We were not to remain calm.

We were not to wait for law enforcement or local authorities to rescue us.

We were not to remain on this station or by any radio and await further instructions. The President expected telecommunications to be down shortly due to military operations being conducted at that very moment. Someone in the back of the crowd watching the TV yelled, "they're gonna use nukes!"

The President told us to do whatever it took to survive, just as he and the First Lady were now being locked in a sealed bunker beneath the White House. He wanted us to do the same, however we might be able to.

You can imagine the general humor at that one.

I thought of an English currency trader I often did business with. He always used the expression "gallows humor", when interpreting his quips over deals gone bad.

Now get this. This was the kicker. It was one of the last things the President told us. I swear he was crying. But he held it together and said it anyway.

"I will not authorize the use of Nuclear Weapons on domestic soil. God Bless America."

At least we didn't have to worry about being nuked. Which meant, at some point they'd actually discussed the option when we were unaware of even the possibility of being nuked. I wonder how close Manhattan had actually come to getting vaporized while I'd shaved that morning, or talked on my Bluetooth on the way to work, or was standing there, watching CNN.

In the future, someone will tell me to think of all the things I have to be grateful for, and I will have to add that one.

Not getting nuked when I wasn't even aware it was a possibility.

And then there was the "domestic soil" fine print you don't even want to get into.

I don't know our new President. He certainly wasn't the Vice. Whatever happened down in that bunker below the White House, I'm sure the President was a standup guy to the end. A straight shooter.

For whatever that's worth these days.

October 28th

It's midnight. Just after. It's been a long day. We're passing through a city. Or, what was once a city. Whole blocks are flattened by fire. You can see the barricades someone tried to put up as everything went to hell. You can smell corpses burning somewhere.

I didn't get to look too long though, thanks to Hanson, the laundry supervisor. Mr. Hanson made us get in and start a series of classes and lectures on how to do laundry the military way and what would be expected of us from now on.

The whole military thing. I thought it would annoy me more than it does. But to be honest, it doesn't.

I even drew the first shift after classes. We started our laundry run at seven this evening, and I ran the steam press, doing sheets until a few minutes ago. Once I learned all the new folds, it became very relaxing. I love the steam. It feels like I'm sweating out all the poison of the past few months. Plus, I had a glass of ice-cold water to drink. As much as I wanted. Hanson, Mr. Hanson, makes sure we get all the cold water we want. It's very hot in there.

When my shift ended, I stood out in the breezeway. There was a sentry out there. We smoked. He told me we were passing through Western Pennsylvania.

We passed through towns where no one moved. All the windows and doors were like more empty eye sockets. Gouged and sightless.

I didn't think much all those weeks in the Tower.

It's now that I'm writing about the Tower, that those long and very hot days within it come back to me and I can smell the carpeted floors and feel the silence of the place.

My Dark Tower.

Sounds sinister once I've written it and see it on the page in front of me.

Let me explain.

After everyone died…

I wanted to use another word for "died". Maybe, after everyone was "murdered". But that doesn't seem right either. The sick didn't know what they were doing. They're little more than animals now.

After everyone died in my little Ka-Tet, as Stephen King would've termed it, there was just me.

Alone in the building.

Every time I cracked a new floor, I was hoping I'd find another survivor.

I never did.

In a sixty-five story building, I never found another survivor besides my fellow co-workers who started out, and didn't finish, with me. Eighty people per floor. Five-thousand two-hundred people per building.

Someone once told me there are over six hundred skyscrapers in New York City.

I used to love numbers.

Roughly three million people in skyscrapers that morning.

One survivor per building is optimistic, considering my trek through the Manhattan wasteland when I went to see what remained of my building. But let's be generous and use me as an example.

One survivor per building.

Six hundred survivors.

Three million, one-hundred and twenty thousand living corpses.

I used to love numbers and all the wealth they could be used to represent.

Now, they make me sick.

After everyone was dead, I spent my days alone in the Tower, rummaging through desks and lunchrooms for enough supplies to keep going. To stay ahead of the tsunami of walking corpses pushing their way up through the stairwells after me. I found things. Even if I couldn't eat them, sometimes, they proved useful.

I found a device full of audio books.

Alone for the last two weeks, I listened to Stephen King's Dark Tower series as I climbed my own Dark Tower, knowing I was running out of floors.

Alone after…

Everyone died.

October 29th

My smoke buddy on the train who guards the breezeway between cars, Kyle, said you can still see them, the corpses, out in the fields. Lone figures stumbling in the moonlight, the passing train almost startling them from their never-ending thoughtlessness. They watch us pass and then begin to lumber and lurch after the train. After us.

Do they stop?

Do they find something new to stalk?

Do they eventually lose interest, or will they follow us all the way to California?

When we arrive, will there be a giant train of them following the rails right into downtown Los Angeles?

Another Holland Tunnel.

Holland Tunnel was bad. I watched a lot of corpses get burned there. So many that I thought I'd seen all the corpses the world had to offer.

I have learned that the world is bigger than you think it is.

I learned that little gem of knowledge while digging out corpses from under the rubble. Or, I should say, I learned that when I lost count of all the corpses I had dug out from under the rubble. It was losing count of the numbers that changed me.

But if you thought about all the people, at the biggest gathering you've ever seen, say the Super Bowl, it's just a fraction of how many people there actually are.

Just the tiniest fraction of the United States.

Which is just a fraction of the world.

Have we even made a dent with all our corpse burning?

Or is there some giant train of sickened dead dragging themselves and all the dead in the world, toward us? This night journey on a train could be just another part of a nightmare that keeps going no matter how many times you wake up and go back to sleep.

So my thinking needs to change.

People killed themselves in the digger camps.

It's a possibility.

The day you get rescued, you're happy.

You made it.

But when you get to thinking, well, you realize you don't have so much to be happy about.

Most likely everyone you know is gone now.

Your family. Brother, sisters, Mom and Dad. Everyone you grew up with. Your first girlfriend. Your baseball team. The guy at the car wash you never said a word to. Your house, or condo in my case, burned to the ground. So all your stuff, is also gone. That career you studied for, worked through internships for, spent every vacation and many late nights worrying about.

Gone.

Stocks and bonds aren't as important as they used to be.

So that's gone.

But you're alive.

Then there are the things you don't think about.

I got a taste of that outside the Holland Tunnel the other day.

Let's be honest, Kathy Henderson-Keil was just a co-worker. But somewhere, to someone, she was Kathy. Just Kathy. And whoever it is, they are desperate for news of her. Desperate to find her.

Well, we found her.

What if it was your big sister? Your Mom? Your Dad?

Riding the bicycle.

These are the things you don't think about.

And then there is Alex.

Does she also fall under "things you don't think about"?

October 30th

The train stopped tonight.

I got off to walk around.

I'm glad to be back onboard now. I'm back inside the sleeper car, writing in my bunk. I have to get up early. I traded shifts so

I could get off and walk around the town we stopped in while our train refueled.

I thought everybody would want to get off. That it would be impossible to trade my shift.

But no one wanted to get off the train.

I thought they were all crazy.

I was waiting in the breezeway with Kyle as the train slowed to a stop. He asked me to find him some smokes in town, if it was possible. He said it wasn't scavenging, according to the rules. Scavenging only applied to personal effects. Not commercial goods as per the latest directive.

"Why don't you come with me?" I asked. "You're the guy with the gun."

He shook his head.

"Can't."

I didn't understand at the time, but I think I do now.

After seeing the town, I think he meant to say "won't" instead of "can't".

The train came into the town fast, crossing over a high trestle bridge at the last minute. We passed barbed wire fences and barricaded buildings at the outer perimeter, as spotlights shot down into the murky darkness of the surrounding forest. I figured we'd be slowing down, but we came in fast, and when the station appeared down the curving line of tracks, brakes screeched and we ground to a halt just inside the station.

Every survivor figured out long ago that corpses are attracted to noise. Most people tend to be pretty quiet now. Back when we were digging outside the tunnel, if some large steel beam had to be moved aside, and when we did, it clanged onto the street as we dropped it, everyone stopped, looking around.

Guilty.

Waiting for them.

But not tonight.

It was cold out and I could see my breath.

I stepped off the train and a sergeant asked me if I was really going to get off.

I said, "Yeah, I am."

I could see he wanted to be glib and say something like, "Well, it's your funeral." But he didn't.

He just said, "We're leaving in forty-five minutes." Then, "I hope you're back on board by then." I could tell he meant it.

There are too few of us left now.

We all need each other if we are going to make it.

The machinegun fire started up shortly after I left the train. It was steady and continuous, coming from the tracks back near the spotlights, echoing out into the dark forest beyond. I started back to the train until I encountered a burly soldier carrying a case that had "grenades" stenciled on its side.

"Is this area safe?"

He stopped.

"Relatively," he said.

"Then what about all that gunfire?" I asked.

"The Zekes have been trailing your train for miles. This area was overrun back during the Outbreak and it hasn't been fully reclaimed. In fact, not at all, really. But don't worry about the gunfire, that was part of our plan. We came in last night by parachute and set up defenses. We'll hold the perimeter until you guys are back under way, then we bug out." With a jerk of his head, he indicated a dimly-lit football field at the local high school up the street. I could see quiet helicopters crouched and waiting as smaller dark shadows moved around them and red lights bobbed up and down.

The gunfire grew louder.

"I'd better get these up to the line, sorry... got to boogie."

Then he was off. Leaving, he called over his shoulder, "Don't miss your train." Then he laughed.

I was alone at the intersection of Main Street and End of the World, Any-Town, U.S.A.

It looked normal. That is, if you didn't look too close.

Looking close you saw the boards tacked up across the windows from the inside.

The bullet holes.

The dark stains.

The splintered boards that had snapped inward.

The open doorways.

The waiting dark.

I felt a brief moment of electricity course up my spine, grabbing at the back of my neck. Standing in the middle of the street, in the middle of the night, the cold turned my breath to steam. I felt like a kid out late, alone for the first time.

I walked down the street, hearing each of my footfalls above the distant echoing gunfire that sounded like some faraway shooting gallery on the other side of a distant canyon rim. A cold breeze crossed the road and felt good on skin that had been too long inside the train and the Tower. I followed the breeze coming from down a deserted street. At the next intersection there were burn marks on the sidewalk.

Something had...

Broken boards blossomed inward across the shattered windows of a nearby grocery store. A few of the boards had turned to splinters, and inside the dark store, survival had taken on a new meaning.

Those people had not made it.

The residential section of town continued on the far side of the street. Barbed wire lay across the next intersection.

I kept on toward the wicked razor wire, strung in circular tangles across the middle of the street.

Was I going to keep going passed the wire and into the fields and the dark night beyond?

As I lay here in my bunk, I wonder now, what was I doing out there?

I didn't have a plan.

There was a part of me that might have been willing to stay there long after the train heaved itself off into the night and the helicopters climbed into the low-hanging clouds. How quiet it would have been at that moment. Quiet, until I heard them, the corpses, out on the perimeter and coming through the wire.

Groaning.

Shuffling forward.

Breaking the blissful night-quiet as they crushed anything in their path and poured over the defenseless defenses.

There was a large house on the corner of that street. It was the kind of house an oatmeal commercial would have been, should have been, shot in. Big and white, gabled roof. Wide porch. Maybe a lemonade commercial.

Boards still covered the broken glass windows and doors on the first floor.

On the side of the wall nearest the intersection, someone had written in large orange spray-painted letters across the white slats.

"TOM HODGES—WE WENT TO THE HOSPITAL. PLEASE FOLLOW."

These people, this town, they had made their last stands. They'd had their objectives just like we'd had in the Tower. Our "get up to the next floor" was their get to the hospital. Just as each floor had successively fallen to a sea of maddened corpses, as we survivors crawled through the communication bundles up into the ceilings, up onto the next floor, so these people had retreated outward.

The safe house down the street.

The supermarket beyond.

The roof of the supermarket above.

The run for the hospital.

The roof at the top of the hospital.

Did a helicopter come and get them, just like I had been rescued? Or was there no place to go after the roof? Was their helicopter hope nothing more than an unfounded wish?

By the time I'd gotten back to the train, the gunfire had increased to that of full-scale war. Explosions came fast and steady, and I thought of the case of grenades I'd seen the burly soldier carrying. Were they being lobbed down into the forest dark, beyond the searchlights, as the corpse people surged forward, mindless of explosive destruction?

I boarded the train and went to my breezeway.

Kyle watched the darkness beyond the lights of the station.

"I didn't find any," I mumbled on the subject of cigarettes.

Voices cried out, as a whistle, literally a train whistle, blew. We were leaving, and the sense of urgency was suddenly dire.

The pale and flickering tube lights of the station went off.

In the dark, the train began to push forward, picking up speed, the familiar clickety-clack returning.

It is a comforting sound.

It means we are moving.

We are not trapped and we can move away from this place. This means a lot to me now. It must also to the others on this train.

I could see flashes of gunfire in the streets of the dead town making a connect the dots game of light that arrived back at the football field and the helicopters whose turbines we could not hear above the noise of the train, as their blades slowly began to turn.

Were the corpse people crawling through the wire as these soldiers who'd set up our refueling point raced back through the streets, envying our moving train as it surged off into the dark.

"That's okay." Kyle handed me a cigarette from his shirt pocket. We smoked, watching the helicopters lift off from Any-Town, U.S.A., as huge explosions erupted in the night sky on the far side of town.

"Napalm trenches to keep 'em back," said Kyle.

The machineguns on top of the train began to chatter away, as the dead came rushing out of the forest darkness and up the small embankment leading to the tracks, grabbing for the train.

Other soldiers began to shoot out into the dark from behind the armored shutters of the train cars or from off other breeze-ways.

Kyle watched the night and I wondered what his story of survival was.

Was he someone's Tom Hodges? Was there a message painted on the side of a house somewhere, written only to him? Was there someone waiting in a hospital or refugee camp for word of their Kyle?

Or was he waiting for someone to find him?

And me?

Was there a message in California for me on a hotel room wall written in marker pen or lipstick?

The terrible numbers indicate I shouldn't engage in such he-licopter wishes.

October 31st

In the laundry today. Too tired.

November 1st

I dreamt last night.

Alex.

I didn't plan to be on this train. But here I am, heading toward California to find Alex after we get there.

If we make it.

Apparently there was another train that left before us. It departed Manhattan two weeks ago. No one has heard from their crew and complement after they arrived in Chicago. So now we're taking the southern route. According to chatter, military talk, Atlanta's our big unknown. Maybe it's our "Chicago". Then there's New Orleans. The word on New Orleans is the Navy will secure a fuel depot just before we arrive. Or so that's the plan one hears in the dining car.

Back to Alex. And California.

At what point in the Tower did I accept she was dead? This was the woman I was going to marry. I loved her.

I love her.

Maybe she left a message. Maybe somewhere in California is a message waiting for me. I know the name of the hotel where she was staying. She was there the last time I talked to her. She sounded distant. But I was distant too. I was going to make a million bucks that day. Same as every day.

Is there a message waiting for me in California?

I could go there and find it.

It's something.

November 2nd

Three days after the end of the world started. That's where my story really begins.

My story is nothing more than four incidents. Four incidents that I must live life with. Four incidents of shame.

My time in the Tower is summed up in these four terrible acts.

Four acts of shame…

It's been three days since it all began.

Three days since those who fled the brokerage disappeared down stairwells and elevators not to re-emerge into the street which was already crawling with the sick. Those who remain, among whom are my little band of soon-to-not-be-survivors, my Ka-Tet, flee up the stairwell to the twentieth.

We leave the nineteenth floor when that wave of sickened, screaming, murderous, once-humans comes ripping through the stairwell door on the far side of the office. It's only by accident that I and Carmichael, a natural leader, Kathy Henderson-Keil, a natural adversary, and Derek from IT, are standing near the stairwell door on the other side of the floor discussing what to do with the victims of Chas O'Neil, who was stark raving mad and whose body is now locked in his office, when that flood of drooling death crashes through our first feeble attempt at a barricade.

We have seen the streets below.

We have heard the last address of the President before the bunker he was sealed in pulled the plug on the outside world.

We'd just killed O'Neil and then locked up the three people he'd torn into, in the conference room. Later, when we looked in on them, through the all-too-thin glass, they were lying on the floor. They looked dead.

Just before the corpse flood, the conference room-ers began to get up and walk around.

We have stayed put. We have sealed ourselves in.

We have locked the doors.

Carmichael holds his bat.

Carmichael's bat.

He always carries it on Monday mornings when we ramp up for the first day of the trading week.

Today he is carrying it for a different reason.

We have seen the bodies in the streets.

On this, the third day, those bodies come roaring through that door on the other side of the floor. We hear that whistling, screaming groan as cheap wood splinters and desks crash over like some giant bird thumping against the windows we once looked out upon our kingdom from.

We survivors have chosen to do what the President said we should do, seal ourselves in, and now we are doomed.

Unless you happen to be standing near the stairwell door on the far side of the floor, discussing what to do with those three corpses in the conference room. The corpses that are now walking around and thumping into the all-too-thin glass partition.

Carmichael raises his bat.

But as they come screaming forward, tearing at a Steve, dragging down a Dana, you know you must run.

And we do, through the stairwell door which we jam shut behind us with a loading dolly, and up to the twentieth.

I think it was a publishing house.

That is the first of my four shames.

That we fled, though there was no other option left to us.

I am ashamed of that.

Atlanta looms in my mind. The laundry will be closed tonight. All of us worked the day shift. Everyone knows something, something very bad, lies ahead of us on the train tracks, waiting for us.

Atlanta is the great unknown.

There is no reliable intelligence or data concerning Atlanta.

Even though it's fall, the air is hot and sticky, as though the last days of this worst summer ever still refuse to say goodbye.

When it rains, will it wash all the dead back into their graves and gutters?

The air is heavy and I have a feeling that something not good waits for us in Atlanta.

November 3rd

This is a record of what I saw in Atlanta.

I know I'm just journaling my feelings and trying to deal with what has become of my life, but I feel I have to put down in words written in a found journal, what I saw. One of the few surviving accounts of the Black Death from the Middle Ages was captured in the diary of some average guy. He didn't know he was leaving the only surviving record of a Plague that wiped out two thirds of Europe. Maybe I'm that guy. Maybe this journal will be all that remains of humanity's grand ambition of surviving our Plague. Maybe. But after Atlanta, I would say surviving this Plague is a very optimistic outlook at this point.

Chances are, we the crew of the train, are the first people to enter Atlanta since the outbreak two months ago.

The train was moving slowly, trying to keep noise to a minimum. All the soldiers were armed to the teeth. Kyle said they had orders not to fire unless the train was attacked directly.

From a distance, Atlanta seemed deserted. No major fires or damage. No smoke. But as we got close, the bloated bodies and clouds of black crows seemed everywhere.

The sick wandered through empty lots and fields in a meaningless and uncomprehending way.

Toward the main part of the city, we encountered a huge crowd of them stacked up against the base of an old bank. I'm talking a Super Bowl-sized crowd.

There must've been survivors inside.

I think everyone on the train thought, for a moment, "We should do something." But what? What were we to do against roughly fifty-seven thousand of them?

The train picked up speed once the crowd began to tear itself away from the bank, chasing after us. Soon we were through Atlanta.

It's not much of an account.

Sorry people two-hundred years from now, but words fail. Even for a man who dug out uncountable dead from the entrance to the Holland Tunnel. Some things are just too much.

If I had to sum it all up for some future generation to understand, I would write this: It looked like a revolution had taken place, and nobody won.

November 4th

Middle of the night.

The train is bouncing its way into the Deep South. All day it has been cloudy, still, thick and hot. Kyle says it smells like hurricane weather.

Lots of excitement today.

I'd been sleeping. It was around two o'clock in the afternoon, when the train began braking hard. We'd done it before when we'd had to remove something that was blocking the tracks. Tension isn't a strong enough word for those long minutes as we waited for whatever it was to be cleared. You feel exposed, waiting for them to come running out of the woods. But they haven't. Not yet.

Today though, the train commander, General Pettigrew came over the loud speaker and announced, "Battle Stations."

I don't have a station, in battle that is. At least no one has told me I have one. So I threw on some pants and went out into the breezeway. Kyle was crouched down behind the sandbags that are stacked there, loading his shotgun. The other soldier, not a very friendly guy, watched the open field on the other side of the train.

On Kyle's side, a small town waited along the tracks. One of those real Southern towns straight out of a movie, or a John Grisham novel. Just a main street, a town square, and a county courthouse.

There were about fifty of the sick stacked up against the courthouse with a few strays wandering aimlessly in the middle of the street. One was carrying a dead cat. I remember that. For a moment, they all paused. As if torn between what was in the courthouse and us on the train. Then one of the heavy machineguns up top began to fire.

There was a bare second where it seemed nothing happened. As if the machinegun were merely firing blanks to get the corpses' attention. Then the dead were ripped to shreds as dark blood and exploding body parts began to paint the walls of the courthouse.

I lit a cigarette and smoked. Now that I write that down, I wonder if maybe that's the reason I can't sleep. Maybe that's another thing I should add to my confessions of shame. A minor confession of shame along the way.

I felt nothing when I saw fifty people ripped to shreds by a heavy caliber machinegun.

But they're not really people anymore.

And it was nothing like Call of Duty.

Down toward the front of the train, a bunch of soldiers exited, scrambling out across high, washed-out, yellow-green grass and up onto the county road running alongside the tracks. One of the sick came running out from behind a building and the lead soldier raised a pistol and dropped him in three shots.

"That's Major Firestein," said Kyle. "Looks like they're going to try to get them people outta that courthouse."

"Got three comin' our way," said the unfriendly soldier, watching the open field on the other side of the train.

"Command," said Kyle into the walkie-talkie on his chest. "This is two-six. We've got contact. Right side, 'bout two fifty out."

The reply sounded as though it came from inside the bottom of an ice chest, on the back of a motorcycle, moving at eighty miles an hour. I didn't understand it.

"Says not to engage until they're right up on us," Kyle tells the other soldier. "Ten meters."

"He's a damn liar," mumbled the other.

The advance party had made it to the front of the courthouse steps. Then they turned and began to fire into the town. I couldn't see what they were firing at.

The other soldier continued, "Major Firestein better git a move on. These three just got real interested. Two minutes tops."

"Don't fire, Atterly," ordered Kyle. "Not until they get within ten meters. Those are our orders."

"Those are your orders," said Atterly.

Back at the courthouse, Major Firestein was shouting into the face of the barricaded door.

"They ain't coming out," mumbled Atterly.

"Just watch them zekes," whispered Kyle.

"Ain't doin' nuthin' but," replied Atterly. "Still, they ain't comin' out."

At first it didn't look like anyone was willing to leave. The courthouse door refused to open, while Atterly called out the diminishing distances between the train and the three "zekes" crossing the open field.

The rumbling whine from the engine began to increase as though the engineer were adding motive power but holding onto the brakes. We lurched forward for a second, and it felt as though we might leave Major Firestein and company.

Suddenly the advance party turned and headed back across the parking lot toward the train, leaving the never opened county courthouse door.

Then the door opened and an emaciated woman came lurching out, stumbling toward the soldiers. The soldiers pointed their weapons at her, yelling for her to remain still. One of the soldiers went forward, and after a moment he gave a thumbs-up, and in the next they were quickly hustling her back across the dry grass and onto the train. They boarded somewhere up front, toward the engine. In the command car.

In the next moment the train was back underway, and for a short time it felt sunny and warm, the heat and humidity purging the poison tension that had accumulated under our skin in those long and taut moments as we'd watched the field and the courthouse door.

I looked back at the receding courthouse. As the train trundled away, quickly gaining speed, I watched as someone inside closed the courthouse door.

Could Alex be out there? Locked up in some county courthouse, waiting? It seems impossible. But today, Major Firestein rescued someone who was waiting for someone else to come along and rescue them.

Maybe the impossible is suddenly possible.

November 5th

I worked in the laundry all day. Then all night. I didn't hear much about our new passenger. I'm too tired to write. I didn't even think about Alex today. I just let it all go. In the breezeway, Kyle and I smoked one cigarette each in the dark with the rushing wind reminding us we were still alive. Before I left, it started to rain big fat wet drops.

Kyle said, "Night," then, "New Orleans tomorrow. Be ready."

For what?

November 6th

The wind picked up in the late morning. We were passing through low-lying bayou country, closing in on New Orleans. On board the train, everyone was quiet. Little conversation was made and truth be told, I came upon a lot of people staring out through the armored shutters as I passed by them along the rocking corridors of the train. Caught, they would return to cleaning weapons or whatever it was they were working on.

In the early afternoon, after lunch, a thin soup and stale crackers, I got called forward to the command car. I was a little nervous. It had to be either some violation of arcane military protocol, or a new job no one else wanted.

I got a new job.

General Pettigrew, a corpulent, red-faced, balding, muscle-bound type with a thick bull neck, called me into his office. He was sweating. That's something brokers notice. There were others standing in the cramped corridor outside his office, signing papers, smoking, stealing glances out the armored shutters.

Inside the office, a converted sleeping compartment, General Pettigrew and Major Firestein welcomed me. Firestein is a pleasant and unassuming man, mild-mannered and slight. He isn't the kind of guy most people expect too much of on Wall Street. But in my experience back on the Street, I found those guys could be the great white sharks you needed to watch out for, or do business with. I figured Firestein fell into that category.

"I hear you like to go walkabout?" opened Pettigrew in a sing-song tone I'd come to know all too well over the loudspeaker.

"Excuse me?" I asked. I wasn't sure what he'd meant and I wondered if I'd done something wrong, committed some serious error. Was I about to be thrown off the train into a field full of… well… the not-so-dead?

"I hear you like to go walkabout. That's how they say it down in Australia. Walkabout."

"No. I don't think I do."

"Hmm. My sources, intel we in the Army call it, tell me you departed the train and walked, unaccompanied and unarmed, through the town of Bradley. Is that not correct?"

"I did," I said, confused. "But, I asked for permission from some sergeant. He told me it was my choice. He didn't recommend it, but he said I could do what I wanted."

"He was right, in that it was not advisable, and also in that he could not stop you."

"Have I committed some infraction?"

"No, not at all. Quite the contrary, you've recommended yourself for the little adventure our dashing Major Firestein has planned for New Orleans."

"I have?"

"Yes. You have indeed. Major Firestein, please explain to Mr. Hamilton how you intend to get yourself and Specialist Mc-Knight killed along with this civilian."

Major Firestein stepped forward and shook my hand. It was both warm and confident.

For a moment he stared at me. Then he took out a cigarette case and a lighter, offered me one, and lit our cigarettes. General Pettigrew coughed and sat down, pouring himself a glass of cold water and mopping the sweat from beneath his jutting chin.

"How did you survive?" asked Major Firestein.

I don't know who will read this journal someday. I don't know if they will understand the nature of the times we found ourselves in during the Plague. They'll probably refer to it as the Catastrophe or the Dead Plague or something along those lines. And while they might understand the facts better than I ever will, especially with the hindsight of history to assist them, there will be some things they will never understand. The question of how one survived is simply not asked. It is not polite. How one survived is best not discussed. There's a sense of shame about surviving. This question is just never asked. It hadn't been asked of me in the two weeks I'd spent in the digger camp and it hadn't been asked on the train. I never thought, in fact it never occurred to me, that anyone would ever ask me how I'd survived.

Why?

Because I don't know the answer of how I survived. I just did, despite myself.

I didn't say anything.

I wasn't trying to be tough or sullen or wounded. I sincerely wanted to help Major Firestein. But until that moment, I'd never expected anyone to ask me that question.

As I write this, I wonder why we're all not asking that question day and night. Until that moment, I didn't have an answer. I had never formulated a response.

Then I said, "I just did."

Major Firestein thought about that for a moment as he drew on his cigarette and exhaled through his nose. Then he seemed to nod to himself.

"Tonight," he began, "as we cross into the shipyards, we'll be refueled by a Navy destroyer carrying diesel. The destroyer's crew is at half compliment and can't hold the docks effectively. When this expedition was planned, we were told the Navy, in force, would secure the shipping area so we could refuel. The weather outside is turning bad. At sea, they're riding out a Category Three hurricane. The destroyer will barely manage to get in ahead of the storm along the coast. Once they refuel us, their future is uncertain."

He lit another cigarette and stared down at a map on the General's desk for a moment. New Orleans lay rendered in street level detail.

"Tonight as the train takes on diesel, I and Specialist McKnight are going to secure a vehicle and drive into New Orleans in an attempt to draw the infected away from the refueling rendezvous. Specialist McKnight will drive. I hope to get a Humvee operational at an abandoned National Guard command post that was reported to have been set up southeast of the city. If there is a mounted gun, I'll operate that. I need one more person to operate a portable sound system to draw their attention. I was hoping that might be you."

I looked at the map Major Firestein was resting his finger on. It meant nothing to me. If it had been the Journal, I could have made sense of it.

I thought about my four shames. I thought about running toward the stairwell door and the things that would happen in the days to follow as we climbed the Tower. I thought about those things even when I didn't want to think about those things, and I was hoping, dreaming, that someday I might stop thinking about those things. Thinking about shame. Someday, maybe I will have other things to think about.

I thought about Alex and the kind of man she thought I was.

"Yeah," I said. "Whatever you need."

Which was my way of saying, yes, I will go with you on your crazy mission tonight.

The wind and the rain are lashing the side of the train in thick sheets. At times it feels as if we might even be pushed off the tracks.

It's almost dark.

We're almost there.

November 8th

Back on board the train. Or, what's left of it.

I just got my stuff from my bunk, aft of the laundry car. Now I have a bunk located in the command section. Apparently I'm Major General Pettigrew's new personal valet. Which is not good. Pettigrew isn't all there. Which is not saying much these days. Most people, after what they've lived through, are not all there. But Pettigrew has a little less than many, many others.

I think Major Firestein is dead. Probably Specialist Mc-Knight also. He was bleeding pretty badly the last time I saw him. Once the dead got inside the window of the Humvee, they were all over McKnight. And of course they went for the last train car, the caboose we call it, once we got back to the train. Though it's not really a caboose in the old-fashioned sense. It's just the heavily-armored rear of the train. Or, it was the heavily-armored rear of the train.

Firestein and McKnight were in the caboose.

So they're probably dead.

Whoever you are that's reading this, I'll bet you're totally confused, so I'll back up a bit and try to put it all down on paper.

Here goes.

We were approaching New Orleans last night. We, Major Firestein, Specialist McKnight, and myself, were up front in the engine, watching ahead for a crossing where a drone flyover had spotted an overrun command post set up east of the city in the first days of the pandemic. The drone had spotted some parked Humvees and McKnight was supposedly a genius at getting vehicles operational.

The rain had let up.

Someone said we were in the eye of the hurricane now.

They also said it was just a Cat Two, but for a while, it seemed as though the train might drive off the tracks at any moment. Then it got quiet and still. Even the swamp grass out on the bayous we passed over stood straight up in the darkness. The bayous looked like silver roads in the cloudy moonlight.

We passed a shot-up sign indicating Miller's Bayou, and Major Firestein said we were getting close. The train began to slow out over a long expanse of bridge. Ahead, we could see New Orleans in shadowy silhouette. It looked like the mangled gray fingers of the recently dead erupting through the carpeted floors back in the Tower, after the power had gone out.

On the other side of the bridge, the train stopped and we ran to the Humvees parked there three months ago on a hot summer day as the world ended.

Major General Pettigrew was already barking over the walkie-talkies at Firestein before we'd even reached the vehicles. McKnight soon had the hood up and some equipment out. Within a minute, the engine of one Humvee fired, spewing black smoke across the chalky road.

I was carrying the sound system. A boom box.

"Gun's empty, check the others for belts," Firestein ordered McKnight. I could smell the lubricant he was coating the gun with as I sat in the passenger seat and waited. I turned on the power to the boom box, awaiting the order to press play. Which apparently was my sole function in this little adventure. Suffice it to say, I felt useless.

McKnight loaded ammo containers into the back of the Humvee as Firestein attached a belt of ammunition out of one and fed it up into the big gun atop the vehicle.

"Okay thumbs up, let's move. Follow the road," ordered Firestein.

The train crawled forward on cue, without hesitation.

"Put your NVGs on, Specialist McKnight," Major Firestein ordered, as he strapped the goggles around his own head. Then he muttered, "check," and scanned the horizon, pulling a knob back on the gun. I heard a loud click as the belt-fed ammo jerked upward slightly.

The inside of the Humvee smelled dusty.

"If it's all the same, sir," said McKnight, "I drive better without those things. Light's real good right now anyway."

"Whatever works best for you, specialist," mumbled Firestein.

Now we were following the road, keeping pace with the train as it struggled back to speed.

"You want me to push play?" I asked Major Firestein.

"I'll tell you when, Jason. Relax and try to pretend we're just going for a drive tonight."

Knowing there would be a "push play, Jason" coming shortly, felt like the anticipation one experiences when the doctor says "this is going to pinch." That "push play" was probably going to be something very real. Something I hadn't seen since the Tower.

Something I'd hoped never to experience again.

We were entering the outskirts of New Orleans now. Empty gape-toothed buildings gazed in stunned silence at the gray lifeless urban-sprawl as we peeled away from the train, heading toward the levee.

The plan was for the train to take on fuel from a Navy destroyer that had come down a large canal. We would prowl the streets, then link up with the train at the rail yard in the city. If the rail yard was under attack, we'd meet the train on the far side of the city.

The first contact came within moments.

We turned down a main thoroughfare of tightly packed two-story buildings, balconies and black wrought iron, and about four of the infected were meandering across an intersection halfway down the street. When they heard our engine they stopped, almost swooning it seemed, and then began that lurching walk-run toward us.

Major Firestein yelled, "Contact, twelve o'clock," and opened up with a burst from the gun that cut all four to shreds once he had their range.

"Advance at half speed, Specialist," ordered Firestein. "Let's see if we can draw more of them out into the open."

Halfway down the block, we came to an overturned car where one of them was trapped inside and snarling ferociously at us.

When Firestein didn't shoot it, McKnight asked, "Aint'cha gonna do him, sir?"

Firestein said nothing and McKnight kept driving.

"Contact nine o'clock, Major," called out McKnight.

"Watch our front, Specialist. Engaging."

I didn't see how many, but I heard them snarling above the repeating thud of the big gun.

"Clear left," said Firestein.

It was at that point the rain started to patter against the windshield.

"At the next intersection, head toward the levee," ordered Major Firestein.

"Roger that, sir," said McKnight.

By the time we reached the intersection, the rain had increased. It was now coming down in brief spasms across the road.

"Sir, it's getting bad. I need to stop and get my night visions on."

"Roger, Specialist. Stop in the center of the intersection and be quick about it."

We stopped as McKnight fumbled down on the floor for his night vision goggles.

"You want a pair? Brought two jes' in case."

He handed one pair to me and I began to put them on.

I told him I couldn't see anything. He told me to hold on.

That's when the shooting started. Right before, Major Firestein in that matter-of-fact, calm, cool, and very collected voice said, "Multiple contacts. Get us up the street to the canal."

Blind, I felt the vehicle lurch forward and accelerate.

Firestein was firing in short, loud, hectic bursts.

"What's going on?" I asked.

"Turn your damn goggles on!" yelled McKnight.

I felt the face and sides of the goggles until I encountered a knob and turned it. The world burst into bright green and fuzzy white.

"We've got 'em in front of us, sir!" screamed McKnight. "They're cuttin' us off. The damn things are trying to trap us."

"Just go through 'em and head north along Canal Street. Specialist, stay calm."

What I saw...

What I saw...

If you lived through it, then you know exactly what I saw.

I saw people. People who were once people. Post-human people.

Dead people moving.

Going down beneath the front of the vehicle as McKnight drove right through a crowd of them.

Hot brass shells cascaded down onto my shoulders, burning me.

But I didn't care.

I saw a woman, gaunt-faced and hollow-eyed, come careening off the sidewalk as she stretched out one blackened claw toward us.

Their eyes, when you look at them with the night vision goggles, don't reflect light. They look like two black pieces of coal.

"Canal Street is clear, sir. Left or right?"

"Left," answered Major Firestein between thuds of machine-gun fire.

At Canal Street I saw two things. Water sloshing over the top of the levee as wind and rain came down onto the shining pavement, and those things pouring out from every door along the street. Hundreds of them came lurching out onto the sidewalk, groaning as they fell toward us.

McKnight swore.

"Move!" shouted Major Firestein, as he swiveled the gun forward and began to rake the passing crowd with machinegun fire.

A vehicle-mounted machinegun does terrible things to the post-human body on a rainy night.

Boarded up shop windows and building facades splintered to pieces as once-vital people were flung back in sprays of fuzzy white and dark green gore against the sides of bone-white walls and night-greenish buildings.

McKnight raced forward, trying to beat the cresting wave as they lumbered out into the street ahead. There was a thin gap of open space closing fast against the wall of the levee.

The gun made a loud clunk and went silent.

The dead crowded into the street ahead, as McKnight gunned it into a thicket of arms and horror-ravaged faces, groaning and gnashing their teeth. Hate seemed to transmit itself through their rictus-clenched smiles.

The vehicle began to skid sideways on bodies.

"Hang on to it Specialist, and get us somewhere I can reload."

McKnight said nothing and seemed to be mumbling to himself, talking his way through yet one more horror.

When is a horror one horror too many?

When have you had enough?

There are only so many floors to the Tower and even Stephen King's Roland must reach the top.

"Jason." Firestein was bending down, hanging onto the hatch with one hand, touching my shoulder with the other.

"Still with us?" he asked gently. As if I was being inconvenienced by all this heroic military effort on behalf of myself and humanity. As if this might be something other than one of the top three horrible moments I have ever witnessed. Still with us?

Where else could I go?

I would go there if I could.

I would go there and I would hope it would be a place where Alex was. That if I could just have Alex on the other side of this, I could survive.

I loved her. I thought I loved her enough to marry her. To spend the rest of my life with her. To give up the single life and start a family with her.

I thought I loved her enough to do that.

Now I realize I love her more than I ever possibly could have imagined in the world that existed before all this.

If, on the other side of all this, I could hold her...

"Still with us?"

For a moment, I wasn't. I was in a future. A future that was perfect for just a moment. A future that wasn't here. Now.

"Still with us?"

I nodded as we shot out onto a clear street.

"Going left sir, back into the city."

"Roger that, Specialist."

Firestein was feeding more ammo into the gun.

"How much longer till they're ready to go, sir?"

There was a pause.

"Another thirty minutes."

"I don't want to be a hero, sir," said McKnight. "But we can't drag that crowd back to the train. Believe me, Major, I do not want to be a hero when I say that."

"Message received, Specialist. Hook right... up there, and let's head north slowly. That main group needs to get away from the rail yard. That's south of our position now. Head back up to Canal and we'll see if we can get them to chase."

On Canal Street, in the darkness, the mob surged forward as water spilled over the levee, knocking some of them down in great sloppy washes. The wind sliced off the lake, driving spray into the crowd.

"Push play now, Jason."

I did.

Major Firestein fired three short bursts into the crowd and they lurched forward toward us.

"Head up Canal slowly," ordered Major Firestein.

For the next thirty minutes, we played heavy metal music and lured the growing crowd farther up Canal Street, heading into the suburbs north of the city.

It was later, when we noticed the side streets clogged with streaming waves of walking corpses, that we knew we weren't going to make the rendezvous.

"Major, how we gonna get back?" asked McKnight above the music and the engine.

"We'll link up with a state route and try to follow the train out of the city. Once we get to a clear area, the train will pick us up."

And that's what happened. It took six hours, but sometime around three in the morning, we found ourselves ahead of the train, sitting in the quiet of a lifeless small town by the side of the tracks. Waiting. We turned off the engine and Major Firestein handed out cigarettes. We watched the darkness and waited.

In time, we saw the light of the train weaving across the land from the east. At one point, it cast a long white light out over a dark bayou.

The storm had moved off and the sky directly overhead was clear. Clouds hung like glowing white billowy curtains across the night sky.

It was the sound of screeching metal that told us something wasn't right.

We heard a loud BANG. Then the screeching got worse. When the train heaved around the long curve leading to the town, we could see an old pickup truck being pushed forward in front of the locomotive.

"Someone must've left a vehicle on the tracks. Idiots!" cursed Major Firestein.

We could hear the radio chatter from Major Firestein's earpiece.

"They're going to stop and try to push it off to the side. Specialist, help with the tow chain in back… turn on the headlights first."

Then Firestein spoke into his mic.

"Command, do you see our light? Stop here and we'll attach the tow chain from the Humvee and drag the truck away from the front of the train."

More radio chatter.

"Be ready boys, they're drawing lots of infected out from the swamp, due to the noise of the brakes and the pickup. This is going to be very close. Jason, when the train gets here, I want you to get out of the vehicle and head to the engine. Get on board quickly. I'll cover you with the gun. You've done enough, son."

I had that "this is going to pinch" feeling.

The squealing the train made grew louder. So loud, I felt it couldn't get any louder, and still it got louder.

"Sir, they're coming out of the buildings!" yelled an agitated McKnight.

We'd been so focused on the train, we didn't notice that many of the dead were already shambling down the street toward us.

Not many. Mostly singles. But it was something we didn't need right now.

Major Firestein began to engage them with the machinegun, knocking down as many as he could. Still, they crawled forward or just got back up and continued toward us as more bullets smashed into them.

The train screeched to a halt in the center of the town.

"Move forward, Specialist, and pull alongside the pickup. Point the vehicle away from the train."

We did, and once we were in place, I waited for the Major to tell me to go.

From the back of the train, tracer rounds and gunfire were zipping off into the woods surrounding the town, as a ragged wave of Infected emerged out of the night-misted bayous.

"Go, Jason! Get on the train now!"

I ran forward.

All I could hear was the THUMP THUMP THUMP of the machine gun as it ground out short bursts against the shuffling, groaning sick that closed in on us from every direction. Between bursts, I could hear McKnight swearing as he dragged the tow chain out of the rear hatch and attached it to the crumpled pickup truck.

Infected were surging around the armored rear of the stopped train.

Grenades exploded.

Every gun cackled on full automatic, stitching wet thumps into the swarming corpses.

The engineer hoisted me up with one hand, and I heard the Humvee gun its engine.

I heard tearing metal.

I heard the engineer swear as he added power, causing the engines to spool up into an urgent doomsday hum.

At first we were barely moving. Then we slowly began picking up speed.

My heart nailed the wall of my chest like a jackhammer.

I saw the dead crash into the side of the Humvee, tearing and hissing. Major Firestein climbed out of the top hatch and dropped off the far side of the vehicle, away from them. A moment later, McKnight flung open the passenger door and pulled away from one of the things that had managed to crawl in after him. They were both running for the rear of the train. I could see McKnight clutching at a blood-spurting wrist.

And then the train seemed to pick up incredible speed all at once. I looked out the rear window of the engine and saw the last few cars falling behind. At first I thought it was an optical illusion. Then I saw the gap between the last cars and the main body of the train widening.

The engineer picked up the phone as a red light flashed urgently telling him he had a call. After a moment he hung up, pushing a long lever forward as the pounding noise of the engine increased and finally drowned out all other sound.

"General wants more speed. Alright buddy, more speed it is," growled the engineer as if someone else was listening, but really, it was only to reassure himself.

The train crashed forward into the unknown night ahead.

I sat on the floor, my back against the vibrating wall of the engine.

We had left our own behind.

Major Firestein and Specialist McKnight among them.

Surrounded in the middle of the night, trapped in a train going nowhere.

Did they have enough ammo?

Since then, things have been weird.

It took me a day to stop shaking enough to be able to write this down. I feel hollow and angry all at once.

I wish there was a place where I could find Alex. A place I knew where to look and knew for sure I would find her. Like a long cross-country drive nearing its end, knowing as you cross those last vast miles, knowing in the deepest place of your heart, that when you arrive, there will be food and comfort and people who love you for no other reason than that they do.

But I don't think there's any place like that left in this world anymore.

November 9th

Yesterday, I thought Pettigrew was going to be a problem.

But in the middle of the night a group of soldiers stormed his office, shot him in the foot, and threw him off the train, somewhere in the darkness we're now speeding through.

I don't even know where we're at.

I thought Pettigrew would be a problem.

Now the mutineers are the problem.

In fact, the entire train is now full of mutineers. If that's what they're called. Some Sergeant named Calloway tried to maintain order. He said we were going to continue the mission and see it through to Los Angeles. He said he couldn't serve under Pettigrew anymore. Not after what happened to Major Firestein.

Apparently Pettigrew had been acting peculiar all along. But we didn't get much of a chance to notice that back in the laundry. The straw that broke the camel's back was stranding Major Firestein and the other soldiers in the caboose. Pettigrew, getting reports that the rear cars were being overrun with infected, had ordered his men to detach the rearmost train cars, stranding their comrades.

They did it, but found they couldn't live with it.

By the next evening, they'd recovered from the shock of what they'd been ordered to do. They simmered long enough to decide they'd need to administer the justice Pettigrew deserved.

Now he's out there. Among them. Running and hiding with a bullet in his foot. So, limping and hiding is more like it. The mutineers effectively sentenced him to death. Or something worse.

If they knew what I'd done back in the Tower to save my own skin, would they throw me off the train too?

Probably.

Do I deserve it?

Yes.

And no.

I deserve it because if I write it down here and let you read it, whoever you are, you'll tell me I deserve it. See, right now, no one knows what I did. No one knows what it took to survive, climbing upward every day, leaving barricades, clearing floors, scavenging. Again and again. Over and over. Ignoring the groans and roars and constant banging of rotten flesh on hollow stairwell doors below you. At times, they seemed so intent at getting to us. Other times they remained quiet. Then, just one of them would start bashing into an object repeatedly, keeping time like some clock in the hall. Like some clock in hell.

Then they'd come after us again.

And I did whatever it took to survive. Even if that meant someone else might not make it.

That's the question. Do I deserve death or worse for making it?

I survived.

I survived long enough to make it to the roof.

To make it to the helicopter.

Through all those floors.

And friends.

The smoke and the wind at the top of the Tower on the day they rescued me felt like just punishment. It felt like Hell's front door. Like being embraced by judgment for the first time, and for all time. And then the Army pulled me off the roof with all of the dead below, clambering up through our barricades. My barricades.

I'd cheated them. The Dead. And judgment.

November 10th

Calloway has lost control. Most of the soldiers are drunk. I went forward to the engineer's compartment to see why we were going so fast. They've forced him to keep the train at speed during the day. We're roaring into Texas now, headed for San Antonio.

No one knows what's supposed to happen in San Antonio.

There was a plan. Maybe another Special Forces refuel mission. But that went out the door with Pettigrew, and Calloway won't let anyone call back to Manhattan on the Sat Phone.

So the plan is just to get to Los Angeles, fast.

I went back to the laundry. No one was working. People are still turning in their sheets though. So I got the machines going and worked for a while. At first I hoped everyone would sober up and go back to work. Stop drinking, playing cards, fighting, and shooting out the window every time we pass a great migrating wave of the sick.

But no one did, and the immensity of the task overwhelmed me.

Finally I just turned on the steam press and pressed one set of sheets over and over. Again and again.

I like steam.

I like drinking cold water while I steam press.

I shared a smoke with Kyle in the breezeway. He hasn't left his post. I guess Atterly was in one of the cars that got left behind with Major Firestein.

I've been thinking all day about what I need to do next.

Which is kind of funny, being on a train full of people suffering from some form of Post-Traumatic Stress Disorder. Or even just being on a train. Because there's not much you can do on a train. Your choice is pretty much made for you. All you can do is wait until it stops.

But I've found something I can do.

I can write it all down. Write down what it took to survive. Then, whoever reads it can judge me.

Maybe I'll just find a stranger in L.A. Just walk up to him or her, and say, "Could you read this and tell me if I deserve to die? If I've somehow done the un-doable thing that we won't be able to live with. Please let me know so I can turn in my human card."

Or maybe I'll find Alex and she'll read what I've done.

And then she can judge me.

November 11th

It's just after three in the morning. I didn't finish the other entry too long ago, but I can't sleep and someone's playing a Neil Diamond's greatest hits CD in the forward compartment. It sounds like there's a party in there.

But that's not why I can't sleep.

I can do it in batches. I can tell you about my four shames in batches. And the truth of the matter is, I've already told you one of them. The shame of running when there was nothing I could do but run.

When it all started, I ran.

And then there is my second shame.

The shame of Derek.

Derek is the guy you never really know when you're a broker. He's the guy who keeps your computer running. But I thought I knew Derek. I always hooked Derek up with a bottle of top-shelf Scotch during the holidays. Well, I did once. We only had one Christmas before things went bad. It wasn't until later, when it was just the four of us in the Tower, that Derek told us he didn't drink. We'd found someone's vodka. It had been a week since everything went sour. A week of going floor to floor, barricading the floor we were leaving, both stairwells with all the desks, cabinets, and shelves we could fling down into the darkness. Knowing that if help didn't come, we'd have to go through the ceiling again in a few hours, or maybe a day or so.

Derek showed us how to get through the ceilings because the dead were filling the stairwells and the floors below. As an IT guy, he knew all about ceilings.

On the night we found the vodka, we'd just made it to the twenty-seventh floor I think. It always felt like a new start each time we burrowed our way through the ceiling and sliced open the corporate carpet with a box cutter, or banged out a wall panel as we crawled up through a telecom bundle. It always felt like starting over as we reached a pristine, almost untouched new floor.

We started drinking after we set the barricades at each stairwell. We found the big offices, searched the desks, pulled the couches together, and stretched out to listen to music on our iPhones. The city, or at least our building, still had power, so we could charge our phones.

In fact, when you looked out the windows at night, the buildings that weren't burning still had their lights on. You could see other people beyond the windows. Other survivors.

There were some people in another building we waved at every night. Their building was opposite ours across an intersection. They couldn't figure out how to get up through the floors like we did. We kept going up and they kept waving at us from below.

Then one night, the survivors in the other building were gone. They didn't come to the window to wave. But there was still movement on their floor. Shadows lumbering aimlessly down the hallways. I thought back over our day. However we'd spent it, it had probably been their last.

That night, we found the vodka and drank it. Each of us laying on our backs, listening to something mellow, we passed the bottle one to the next. Then I realized Derek wasn't drinking. Hadn't been drinking. He'd just hold the bottle for a moment, then pass it on. Carmichael next, I think. Kathy, Derek, Carmichael, then me. Repeat.

I asked Derek why he didn't drink. He said he just didn't. He said drinking was his apocalypse. In college he'd had a problem. He'd quit. Gone to AA. But in the back of his mind, he'd always had what he called an "Apocalypse." A dark fantasy that took place if life went completely sideways on him someday. Then he'd drink again.

I asked him what "sideways" meant. As in, what are the terms of the deal in which one finally announces things have gone officially "sideways".

He was quiet. "Don't know," he said. "I'll know when it happens." Then he added, "Family dying stuff. My wife getting killed in a subway accident. That's sideways."

Yeah. I know. It's obvious. If anything was ever going

to be considered "sideways", our present circumstances in the Tower would definitely qualify. I didn't even know he had a wife. I couldn't imagine she was still alive out there somewhere. I couldn't imagine anyone was still alive besides the four of us.

Sideways.

Three days later, two floors above, Derek opens an office door and one of them comes straight for him. All of us were checking offices in the same hall.

We always found booze.

Derek pushes it back into the office and closes the door.

Then Carmichael goes in after it with his Monday morning meeting bat.

He's screaming at it. Working up all the Alpha Male stock-broker rage he needs to bash another one into…

I look at Derek.

He's bleeding.

At that moment, I'm thinking something I never thought I'd ever think.

I am not thinking, "How can we save Derek?"

I'm thinking, "How can we get rid of Derek?"

We are going up to the next floor, Derek. You can't come.

But I don't say anything at just that moment.

Kathy doesn't say anything either. She just looks away as if Derek no longer exists.

Carmichael coming out of the room, heaving, looks at Derek and says, "Walk it off, bro."

Like Derek just got beaned by a stray pitch in the Big Game.

Not bitten by a rabid human corpse.

Later that night, when Derek helps us move up to the next floor, as Kathy is handing things we've collected up to Carmichael, Derek says, "the truth is, I don't have an apocalypse."

Then, as if I hadn't heard him, Derek says again, "I don't have an apocalypse, Jason."

I stare at him. Because though no one has said it, no one has actually articulated it, we are leaving him down here. It was his idea to move on to the next floor up. Except he's not going, and he knows it.

"My sponsor," he says, still talking, hoping we're listening, "is this old guy. So old they call him the Crocodile. He said to me one time, don't ever have one. Don't ever have an Apocalypse. He said that to me when we weren't even talking about anything in particular. We were just sitting together at a diner over on 54th. Having coffee, taking inventory. I was good, so there wasn't much inventory. I was watching the traffic while I told him about something I occasionally thought of and felt bad about. I told him that if Monica, my wife, ever got killed, like pushed onto the subway tracks, then I'd get all the tequila in the world and I'd just drink it. Right there in that coffee shop, I... I fantasized about what it would be like. If my wife was dead and I could drink as much as I wanted to again. And this wasn't a long fantasy. It was real short. Like, in the time it takes you to blink your eye, you see the whole dark picture. My sponsor just says, he's staring out the window too, watching the traffic, he just says, "Don't ever have one."

"One what," I say.

"An apocalypse. Don't ever have an end of the world just so you can start drinking again. Because chances are, kid, you'll live long enough and you'll get your apocalypse, and the last thing you'll need to do is start drinking again."

We didn't say anything. But Derek knew we were listening to him. To his last words.

"This guy was so good at being a sponsor to human wrecks

trying to put their lives back together," continued Derek. "He knew every trick in the book, and I didn't even need to ask him why. I just said to myself, "Okay, I won't have an apocalypse.""

I stared at Derek as he finished.

"In a minute, you're going to go through the floor and before you do, you're going to ask me if I want to keep the bottle we found today."

I was going to. I'd planned on it already. I'd even thought it was pretty magnanimous of me.

That moment with Derek was one of the top three most intense conversations I've ever had. Now that I write it down, I realize I didn't even say a word. I just listened to this guy I didn't really know. But if you'd asked me before all this happened, I would have told you all about him in one glib descriptor sentence. Something like, he's just the IT Guy. I would have briefly summed him up for you that way.

I would have been wrong.

Because, I bought a bottle of scotch as a Christmas present for a guy who didn't even drink.

He was right.

I was, before leaving him to die, going to offer him a half a bottle of vodka we'd found in someone's desk.

"I don't want it," he said. "Because I don't have an apocalypse anymore."

He was already sweating. He looked grey. He didn't have long. But he would've had long enough for the bottle.

Once I was through, we sealed up the hole.

The last time I saw him, he was sitting with his back against a support column. Smiling. Talking to himself.

I am ashamed because Derek didn't have an apocalypse.

And I did.

And I lived through it.

But I had one all the same.

November 12th

We shot through San Antonio at high speed. We didn't even use the brakes. It felt like the train increased its speed beyond what had already been considered irrational as we approached the city. I watched from the laundry, which I have to myself now. The entire city had burned to the ground. In places, it was still smoldering. A big fire off to the northwest sent clouds of dark smoke and ash drifting in waves across the blackened brick and charred stumps of the city. It was like the end of the world.

Corpses, blackened, smoking, some even on fire, wandered aimlessly amongst the ruin.

I thought about being seven years old.

I thought about summer vacation that year.

I thought about the train at Disneyland that passed through all those set piece dioramas.

The Old West.

Dinosaurs.

The end of the world.

Calloway finally called in and radioed our position. No one knows what he said, but he just came out of Pettigrew's office and handed some coordinates to another soldier to take to the engineer. He says we'll be refueled at those coordinates. Then he went back into the office and locked the door behind him.

Things have quieted down. The celebration of the disposal of Pettigrew has run its course. Most people sleep all day, or smoke alone in the breezeway.

And this is odd, but it almost seems like there are fewer people onboard than just yesterday.

Would someone actually jump from a fast moving train?

Or were they thrown?

If I can write down everything and find Alex… find out what became of her… even if it's the mass grave where she's buried, is it wrong to think I could be forgiven?

Once we refuel, it's supposed to be a straight shot into L.A.

November 13th

The laundry's up and running again. I just got off my shift. It's past midnight. I stopped by the dining car and got some tortillas and coffee. I haven't had fresh produce, or fresh anything for that matter, since… before.

I guess if I have anything to look forward to, it is that someday I'll get to eat fresh produce again. I would love to eat a real tomato. With some salt. Smoked salt.

Calloway is dead. He blew his brains out. Sometime last night. The door to Pettigrew's office was locked. They had to break it down. They waited until we'd reached the coordinates. When he didn't come out to see what they'd sent to refuel and resupply us with, someone broke down the door and there he was. I saw him. He looked plain dead. Like people used to look before all this.

He missed the three big C-5 Galaxy transports that landed at an airport next to the train tracks. Fuel lines snaked away from one transport and right up to the train. Cargo and people started streaming out of the transports all at once.

Colonel Powell, the new commander sent to link up with us and take over, didn't like what he found. He arrested a few of the key people and sent them with some other basket cases back onto the military planes. The rest were told to report to their workstations on the train. Now there are more soldiers. Discipline is being enforced and questions are being asked. Everyone's pretty much afraid. But they're back at their jobs. Which is probably for the best. We were looking to get ourselves killed. If we'd run into anything, everyone would have been either too tired, too drunk, or too depressed to fight back.

Powell addressed the train just before the night shift commenced. We were underway and you could smell hot food coming from the dining car. The military transports had roared off into the night above us as the train got up to speed once more.

"It's time to pull it together." That was the gist of Powell's speech that night over the train's PA system. Basically, according to Powell, the U.S. controls Manhattan and most of Southern California. The rest of the country is still enemy territory. There's no cure for the infected, other than death by bullet to the head.

The government is hoping to clear the U.S. by next summer. Until then, everyone is going to have to decide whether they want to live or die. And if they want to live, they're going to have to work.

The next thing he said seemed to make everything that's happened for the last three months seem normal and what was coming, truly crazy.

I guess, according to Powell, we may have to invade California.

It seems California fared better that the rest of the world, regarding the outbreak. Now there's a civilian government in California that's not so crazy about following the new President's orders. So, if push comes to shove, apparently Powell and his men are to restore California and ensure its place in the union.

Crazy, huh?

November 17th

The invasion didn't go so well.

I haven't had time to write until now. Now that the train has been derailed and the Army is trying to figure out how it's going to invade Los Angeles, there's a little time to write.

We're in Riverside. Riverside, California. It's been a windy and warm afternoon. Lots of blowing sand. The evening should be cool. I've collected some gear, along with some that was issued to me. I think Powell and his men assume all of us civilians are going with them.

I'm leaving. I'm waiting until dark, and then I've found a neighborhood I can slip through and get away from the little fort they've set up around the derailed train cars.

They've even raised an American flag.

I really don't think this is the time for people to get political. It's time to survive, or die. And I'm not sure which one I want yet, but the Army and I have gone as far as we're going to go together.

I feel like a deserter, but I never really joined.

Still, I'm leaving.

My goal is to get to L.A., which I'm guessing is secure, and then make my way down to Newport Beach and find Alex's hotel. I'm writing everything down in case I can't tell her, then maybe she'll read it. Maybe she'll forgive me. If she does, then maybe we can have some kind of life together. I could do that. I could have a life again. I could want to live again. If it was with Alex.

I'm talking like she's still alive.

I want her to be.

While I wait for darkness to cover my escape, I'll write down what happened once we got to Riverside.

Powell had everyone ready for an invasion. No one knew what we'd find here in Southern California. In fact, we expected "here" would be downtown L.A. at Union Station. Then we expected a shooting match, or talk, or something.

Instead, they derailed us in Riverside, sixty miles east of Los Angeles.

They even warned us they would do it. They put up big hand-painted signs telling the train to slow down. We weren't even going fast, when suddenly the engine slid off the tracks and all the cars piled up behind it. For a moment, it felt like we were going over on our side, but we didn't. Then we heard a little plane circling us. When I looked out the window, there were sheets of paper coming down everywhere.

Someone had printed "Now entering the New California Republic. Consider this a warning."

Once everyone was outside the wreck, Powell had us all start "digging in" as he called it.

Yikes, as Alex used to always say.

So now I'm waiting for the sun to go down. It's been a long day, but I'm excited. I want to do this. I'm ready to leave and find what I need to find, Alex, on my own.

November 18th

I started out last night about eight o'clock. I envisioned some kind of mad dash through barbed wire and search lights. There would be yelling and barking dogs. But we didn't bring any dogs. I was sure there would be a barking dog. Nothing.

Instead, I just walked away.

I set out across a field toward a deserted housing development surrounded by a wooden fence.

I climbed the fence and dropped down into someone's backyard.

I was finally all on my own, and alone.

For a moment, I thought about the infected. But we hadn't seen one all day. Not even after the derailment. I thought, at the time, that Southern California was indeed secure. Now I realize it's secure-ish. Maybe.

In the backyard of the big house, a McMansion they called them before the bubble went bust, I felt totally alone.

And I liked it.

The house was dark. I didn't want to go in there. In fact, it was probably best to get moving away from the Army. Headed toward Los Angeles.

I went through the side gate and onto the front lawn. I found a quiet street of similarly-shaped houses. All boxy and large, looming, their windows like eyes that seemed to watch me.

At the tiny intersection of Verde Terrace and Palacio Real, I found piles of burnt ash blowing in the night wind. Skulls lay partially submerged within these piles.

At the end of this mess, how many people will simply be listed as "missing"? Missing forever until there is no one left to miss them.

In the distance, behind me, I could see the searchlights the Army had placed atop the wreckage of the train continuing their slow track across the field where the train had come to rest.

Looking back now, I ask myself, "What was I doing?" I mean, I truly didn't know if the area was secure or not. The ash piles seemed to indicate someone had come through and cleared the area. Rescued those who could be rescued and burned the remains of those who were beyond rescue.

But I didn't know the score.

Standing there amidst the once-manicured streets and empty tract houses of paradise lost, I felt free. Free of the Tower. Free of a seemingly unending climb that would surely end on the roof, or before… if things had gone badly, as they so often did. I felt free of the train that would only go west until there were no more tracks and we fell into the sea or off the edge of the world.

I was feeling poetic in the warm night wind sweeping off the deserts of San Bernardino and all the deserts we had crossed to get here. I felt free looking at the odd skull grinning up at me from the ash.

I felt free.

I would find Alex.

Until that moment, it'd just seemed like a dream, or a hope one tells oneself to keep moving, to eat another bowl of tasteless rice and beans, to dig more corpses out from underneath the overpass outside the Holland Tunnel Battleground, to not give up. I had said it at times amidst the steam of the laundry and the cool of the breezeway and thought, like most do when making bold plans, that it was a true statement. So true, I might never need to live up to it.

But I had escaped the train and the Army.

I could make any promise, and break any promise, if I chose. And it seemed possible, at that moment, to do anything.

Which was something I hadn't felt since this all began.

At the end of the street, I might have found more of the sick, waiting and hungry, a surprise as they turned the corner and came for me. Where can I run that has not yet been run to? Where can I hide that has not already been discovered?

Nevertheless, at that moment I could go on.

I could find Alex.

My awakened mind of possibilities had neglected, until that point, the tools I'd need to actually survive. Then I noticed something I might take with me all the way to wherever I would find Alex.

There were a few cars along the street. Cars where belongings had been loaded. Cars that had been pried open and their contents spilled out into the street. Dead vehicles left running three months ago. Vehicles requiring keys that had long since been hidden within mass graves or melted in ash piles. Or discovered in some other place where no one would ever be able to link the found key with the missing vehicle that must exist somewhere in what are likely the frozen logjams of our roads and highways. An SUV at a nearby house, door still wide open, bags lying nearby, seemed to be caught forever in the act of waiting to be loaded. An inanimate thing waiting for a lively owner to come racing out the front door with that last forgotten item, on that last never-to-be-forgotten day, as sirens blared and women screamed and children must surely have cried.

On the lawn nearby, a golfer's bag of clubs has disgorged its drivers and irons.

I approached and scanned the scattered sticks.

Whoever owned this bag must have had a serious golf habit. The kind I'd always meant to develop once I'd made the mythical "enough".

I picked up the Big Bertha.

I could take this, I thought. If they, the dead, are still about, this might come in handy.

Yea though I walk through the valley of the shadow of death…

And I had no idea where I had acquired those words. Some half-remembered Sunday school prayer.

Thy rod and Thy staff they comfort me.

With the Big Bertha over my right shoulder, I set out across the silent neighborhood.

I crossed a sea of moonlit neighborhoods forever scarred by

broken glass, vomiting their contents on long uncut lawns, sitting darkly on streets that ended in intersections where ash piles waited and skulls smiled.

At midnight, I came upon an elementary school.

The moon was still out.

I could hear the chime of the tether ball lanyards clanging against metal poles.

I found tiny knee-high drinking fountains against a rough-hewn wall of stone. I drank, and then sat back against the wall and watched the bright moonscape and listened to the lonesome clang of a metal lanyard at the end of a rope hitting a pole in the night.

In the morning, I thought, I should find a map and head toward Los Angeles.

I must have fallen asleep because I woke with a start. The moon had gone down, and for a moment I was frightened as I tried to remember where I was in the darkness. I remembered the escape and finding the Big Bertha that I'd left across my knees. I heard a scraping sound.

Like one foot being dragged behind the other.

I peered into the darkness.

I could see the vague silhouette of a human form shuffling across the basketball courts. I waited motionlessly and silent. The infected were drawn to sound. We'd figured that out in the Tower.

For a moment, the scraping sound stopped and I watched as the figure slowly turned, scanning right past me. Then the scraping began again as the thing continued across the basketball courts and on toward a sandbox where a jungle gym and monkey bars made skeletal shapes in the night.

The figure tripped and fell face forward into the sandbox with a dull thud.

I heard it groan.

Slowly I stood up.

I shouldered my bag quietly and gripped the driver with both hands. I raised it above my right shoulder.

I crept forward across the tetherball courts and onto the basketball court.

My tennis shoes softened my steps, and when I came close, I could see the thing, face down, struggling to get up.

It was missing a foot.

It wore a tattered dress.

Its long dark hair was matted and stringy.

I could brain it now and be done with it.

I raised the club over my head.

Was this someone's mother, their daughter? Someone's Alex?

It didn't seem to notice me. It kept mindlessly flailing about in the sand as it crawled to the edge of the box and then into the field beyond.

I followed it with my club upraised.

Carmichael had always done the killing. He didn't mind. Until the end.

I followed her out onto the night field where children might appear in the morning to play a game of touch football at recess, as girls walked and gathered along the low mesh fence. As if all that might ever happen again.

Before I realized what I had done, I had stopped and the thing had continued off to the edge of the field and the weeds beyond.

I was alone.

I left the school and continued in the direction I had hoped was west. I couldn't be sure. Not until dawn. At dawn, I would get my bearings and find a place to rest. I passed through another tract home development. The remains were different. Here, the people had chosen to fight. Houses were burned. Bullet holes everywhere. Broken glass and splintered plywood. Some had even circled motorhomes into a fort-like structure. One motorhome had fallen inward as if crushed by some great weight. Beyond this lay ash piles and more skulls.

In the dark before dawn, it was cool and quiet. I drank water from the canteen the Army had given me.

A few minutes later, I could hear the birds testing their first songs in the still-dark sky.

I couldn't remember the last time I'd heard birds.

I crossed the parking lot of a big box home improvement store. There were no cars in the parking lot. I stood silently listening to the birds, sipping the stale water in the canteen.

The sky began to turn blue in the east, and I could see the silhouettes of low and jagged mountains.

The big box store looked cold and forlorn.

I felt tired.

I entered the store.

There was hardly anything left.

Every piece of lumber, pallet of bricks, can of paint, and tool was gone.

There was no sign that anyone had put up a defense, and I wondered if the store had gone belly up in the tough economic times that had occurred before the pandemic. Times that now seemed like some lost golden age.

I found a packing blanket lying on a dusty countertop, and shook it out. I climbed on top of some risers to a long flat space where overstock had once waited to be moved to the floor and sold and then installed in someone's tract home castle.

If any of them came in, I would be safe up here.

I went to sleep and when I woke a few hours later, I lay there listening to the birds play in the skeletal rafters above.

Somewhere, today even, I might find Alex.

I blocked out the ash piles and the skulls and the mass graves at the entrance to the Holland Tunnel.

November 19th

I left the empty big box store as the heat expanded the creaking metal roof. It sounded too much like one of them moving around. Stuck on the roof forever.

Outside, I found an iron blue sky and a burning sun. It was hot for late fall. Still, it was California on a map that must exist somewhere.

I went west toward a big interstate off in the distance.

A sign told me it was the 10. I knew from one business trip to L.A. that the 10 ran right through the heart of the city. So I would walk west along the freeway until I reached Los Angeles.

I passed roadside sprawls of urbanized warehouses. Huge long-stretching blocks of massive white box-buildings, empty loading bays, doors thrown open, ash piles inevitably.

When I entered the no man's land that lay between these places, I began to breathe again. I had waited through those long stretches of warehouses for some mass of shambling Infected to come lurching out of the dark openings, rumbling, arms outthrust toward me. But in the emptiness between those places I felt safe, and when I saw a jackrabbit I felt almost normal.

How long will that last? How long will survivors fear abandoned places? How long will these places remain alone and unconsidered?

At four o'clock I heard shooting.

The sky had turned orange, and a cool wind blew off the

desert, drying the sweat between my pack and my back. I stood listening to the shooting on top of an overpass. To the north lay an industrial sprawl where gun shots seemed to bounce off the alleyways that were like canyons between the massive buildings.

When I finally spotted the source of the gunshots, I ducked behind the concrete rail of the bridge.

It was my first reaction.

Didn't I want to be rescued?

I did.

I peered over the barrier and watched them.

There were three men. All with guns. They were near a large off-road truck. Beyond them, a figure twisted wildly at the end of a rope hanging from a tall light post near a warehouse.

The dark shadows of the men in the orange light of the fading day showed them to be reloading their guns, their bodies jerking in distant laughter. The hanging figure, a man maybe, seemed to dangle and flail above them, reaching out claw-like hands toward the shooters.

They began to fire their guns into the dancing corpse. Sudden silhouettes of blood spray indicated hits, while the corpse was flung side to side as if performing some hip new dance. Suddenly it stopped as its head jerked backward.

The men shouted in anger. One threw a hand into the air. The other two held out their hands and the man with his hand in the air shouldered his gun and reached into his pocket, handing each of the others something.

It didn't take much to figure out what that was all about.

I didn't want them to see me. Not those kind of men.

I heard the distant roar of an engine and the sound of wheels churning up dust as the engine gunned louder and louder. I peeked over the barrier and saw their truck turning in a wide circle, raising a front of dust that covered the dangling, motionless corpse.

They drove off into the city of warehouses, and for a while I could hear their vehicle until its sound was faint and then finally gone.

I didn't want to find out what I now needed to know.

Was the corpse an infected? Or was it some traveler like myself? A loner caught by Low Men.

Stephen King's Low Men.

I came down off the interstate and made my way across the weed-choked field, hearing its dry crunch beneath my tennis shoes. When I made it to the light post, I looked up.

The dust-covered corpse was black with necrosis. Its pants were torn, its claws once hands, hung slackly downward, stretching toward the earth. He was well dressed. Or, had once been. The slacks and shirt were business casual. The shoes dress loafers. He looked Hispanic. Clean cut.

I should have killed the woman corpse from last night.

I should have... put her down. Is that right? No one would want this. No one would want the past weeks and months of this disease. No one would want to end as a play thing for the worst kinds of games man can invent. A game to play while the world ends. He who gets the headshot pays. The fun stops with the headshot. So whatever you do, don't shoot it in the head. Let it dance, boys. Let it dance.

I would have cut him down. I would have burned him. But I had nothing to cut with and I had nothing that would burn. So I left him there.

If someone had left Alex, or what was once Alex, like this, then I would find her. I would cut her down and I would burn what was left of her. After that, I could let go.

I feel very alone.

Where is Newport Beach?

November 20th

I am waiting for the bus.

Last night I heard vehicles racing around after midnight. I had climbed on top of an overturned semi lying across the interstate. That was where I slept, badly. It was pretty cold. The night sky was crystal clear and I could see stars like tiny pieces of breaking glass exploding away from me in the blue velvet of deep night above.

Later, it must have been before midnight, I saw headlights in the fields to the north and watched them as they traced the empty streets in a slow convoy, playing their radios loud and gunning their engines. It was like they were trying to draw out the infected. But I didn't hear any gunfire, so they must not have drawn any. After a while, they congregated in an area a mile or so away from me, and their headlights all went off at once. They started a bonfire.

I thought about them all together, waiting in the darkness, together and not alone.

At first light, after what felt like just a few minutes of sleep, I splashed some of my remaining canteen water on my face and got down off the trailer. I walked across hard dirt and uneven fields toward where I had seen the fire. I knew I was close when I smelled smoke in the air and, shortly, the aroma of coffee.

The vehicles were all off-road trucks formed into a wide circle. As I approached, I could see at least one person standing on the roof of each, scanning the horizon. I started to shout and run forward, waving my hands. When one of them raised a rifle and aimed it at me, I shouted, "I'm human! I'm not sick."

As I got closer, they lowered their rifles.

"What's yer name, boy?" asked a kid younger than me, carrying an assault rifle.

"Jason. Jason…" And this is the odd part.

I couldn't remember my last name.

I hadn't used it in so long, I'd almost forgotten it.

"You ain't sick, Jason?" asked the kid.

"No, not at all."

"Got any bites or scratches? Might as well start taking your clothes off, we have to check. It's the law and all."

"What?" I asked.

"Take off yer clothes. We got to inspect yer body. Gotta check for bites, scratches, and the rash. You can tell the infected. Git a rash almost as soon as they come down with it. You got a rash?"

"No. No rash."

"Well, we'll see. Start taking 'em off and don't worry, we ain't perverts." He spat a stream of thick brown juice off to one side of the vehicle he was standing on. "Jes bein' safe. You want coffee while we check?"

"Yeah, I could use some coffee and something to eat, if possible?"

"Yeah, we got it. Git them pants off too."

As I stood there, naked at dawn with twenty men and women watching me, a doctor, at least they called him "doc", and his assistant, came out to check me. The assistant handed me coffee and some fried dough rolled in cinnamon and sugar.

It was the best thing I ever ate.

I'm not kidding.

I have eaten at the finest restaurants in New York and London. But standing there in the breeze, drinking real hot coffee and chewing sweet, fried dough made me feel human for a moment. I started to cry a little, and when I did, I realized how alone I had been out there in the dark.

"He's clean," shouted the doctor, and turned to head back into their perimeter.

"You can git dressed. I s'pect you'll want to come with us, Jason No Last Name. We can drop you at the supply rendezvous this morning and you can catch the evening bus into L.A. Ain't you gonna git dressed?"

I said I would as soon as I finished my coffee and donut-thing. They told me it was called a churro.

So I'm waiting for the bus at the supply rendezvous which is really just a fortified gas station. They have buses pulled around the perimeter and sharpshooters at all four corners.

Riley, the kid with the assault rifle, told me it had gotten pretty quiet out there in the last few weeks. They were mostly in the "clean up" phase now. They didn't suspect many of the infected would migrate across the Mojave Desert and into the populated areas of Southern California. Now they were just cleaning up strays and those that had gotten themselves trapped somehow.

"Found one trapped in a women's restroom at a Mickey-D's last week. Must've been there the whole time. Imagine that," said Riley. And I did.

"Where'd you come from?" he asked me.

"New York."

"New York?"

"All the way."

"How?"

"By train."

"Train?"

"All the way."

"Where's the train?"

"Derailed out in Riverside."

"In Riverside?"

"In Riverside."

"Why?"

"Someone derailed it."

"That'd do it. Why was you on a train?"

"New President sent us here to reconnect with the West Coast."

"Ain't no President here in California. We got a board of Governors."

"How's that working?"

"Sucks far as I can tell." Then, "What happened to New York?"

"I don't know. I was stuck inside my building most of the time. I climbed to the top of it, sixty-five floors, and when I got there I was… there was a helicopter in the sky. They came and got me."

"A helicopter. Ain't that something?"

"It was."

"Then you came west?"

"I did."

"On that train?"

"All the way."

"That's something."

"I guess it is. Do you know where Newport Beach is?"

"Yeah, it's out by the ocean. Just follow this freeway and when you get to L.A., go south on the Five. It'll take you down to Irvine. When you get to Irvine, head west on any of them roads and you'll end up in Newport. Simple."

"Sounds like it. How'd you survive?"

I thought, maybe in California they talk about it.

About surviving.

But I don't think they do.

Riley looked out upon the vast expanse of scrub and highway for a long moment.

"Some days I remember. Some days I don't know how. Some days I don't know why. I got a four year old daughter named Savannah back at base. I had to. It was just me and her. So, you know, I had to."

I understood.

Remember when I told him about surviving in the Tower?

Remember when I paused as I told him I got to the top of the building?

I was going to throw myself off the roof.

I didn't have a Savannah.

Sorry Alex.

I can hear a diesel engine in the distance. I think it's the bus.

November 21st

It's about ten o'clock at night and I'm sleeping in a van, an old Volkswagen minibus. It's part of a welfare hotel for refugees until they get their feet under them. I'm on level eight of a parking garage located beneath the Dorothy Chandler Pavilion on the highest of Los Angeles' seven hills.

I think they used to hold the Oscars here.

Not in the van. Up in the Dorothy Chandler.

Crazy, huh?

I got into Los Angeles late last night. The bus picked me up out in Riverside and then took forever to get to Union Station. The freeway was impassable from the wrecks and traffic jams of two months ago. Long silent trains of cars seemed forever frozen

on the highway. You see a lot of broken glass. It makes you wonder.

When we encountered these impassable barriers, the bus de-
toured off through a break in the highway and trundled along side
streets. The driver, smiling, seemed to know where he was going
as we jounced along listening to Mexican music.

In the early evening, the bus labored up the last streets east of
Los Angeles, crawling along narrow ravines through old neighborhoods where gabled houses stood guard in the twilight. Occasional dim lighting smiled wanly through the gloom. Then all of
the sudden, we're pulling through a makeshift wall into the flickering orange and neon-lit streets of downtown Los Angeles. The
skyscrapers beyond the station are dark, but the streets around
them are illuminated at odd intervals by running generators and
light poles.

Most of the other passengers seemed to know where they
were going, and soon I found myself standing alone as the driver
exited the now silently ticking bus.

"No place to go tonight?" he asked, his Mexican accent thick
and singsong all at once.

I shrugged.

"Hungry?"

I nodded.

"Follow me."

We crossed the street and went down the block toward the
edge of a brightly lit area I thought would be busier, but was
strangely lacking in human presence. At the end of the block, I
saw thin light spilling out onto a street corner. The signage above
the building was dark, and I could barely make out the darkened
Philippe that must have once burned bright and hot in the 1950's
Los Angles nights of neon and chrome.

At the front door, the bus driver, Alphonso as I would come to know him, said one word.

"Chili."

Inside it was quiet. The floor was covered in sawdust and dishes were being cleared from long tables, as though a large group had only recently eaten and left.

We ordered two bowls of chili with onions. Cheese was unavailable, we were told curtly by an older woman wearing a vintage waitress uniform complete with a paper cap. There was pie though. So we ordered pie and two cups of coffee. When it was time to pay, Alphonso held out large multi-colored bills and laid them on the counter. I caught the words "Republic of New California" printed on them.

We ate and Alphonso read a newspaper that was little more than a single printed sheet.

The chili was good, and when we finished the pie, Alphonso put down the sheet and looked out the window onto the dark street.

"The Dodgers are going to play an exhibition game on Saturday."

I said nothing.

"Imagine that," he continued in his thick accent. "I spent six weeks at Dodger Stadium trying to survive just one more day. It was very bad. Now there will be baseball again."

He sighed as he finished his coffee.

"I love baseball," announced Alphonso. "One year I watched every game the Dodgers played."

I nodded approvingly.

"It wasn't a very good year for the team. Still, it felt like I had accomplished something. I felt like a real fan."

"So," I began, and then had to clear my voice. I hadn't really been using it much lately. "Will you go Saturday? To the game?"

For a long time, Alphonso stared out the window and I began to wonder if he'd heard me.

He sighed again, which seemed to be his manner. As if the world and all that was in it were a weight that must be constantly expelled.

"Yes," he said simply. Then, "I will go. I must go."

There was more to the game on Saturday for this man than just the score and perhaps seeing a home run go out over the left field fence.

I thought of Carmichael and his Monday Morning Meeting Bat.

I knew that somehow Alphonso's going to the game would be an act of defiance. I saw him sitting in the bleachers, not really watching the game. Merely remembering those six weeks that were the end of the world. He would sit and he would cheer when he must, and buy a hotdog if they had them, and maybe even a beer. In the end, as the light faded and the fans returned to their bunkers, no longer fearlessly roaming the night streets as they once had, Alphonso would smile, congratulating himself that "they" did not beat him. I don't know how, but for a moment I felt I could read his mind, and that was exactly what he was thinking. That was his dream, or simply, that was what he knew he must do to go on living.

We left and walked through the rubble of what, Alphonso turned tour guide, told me had once been the historic district. Bricks lay scattered in great sprays across the streets and soon, as we neared the brightly illuminated and silent freeway, we crossed over into downtown and walked up a hill, passing a modern new cathedral where candles guttered in the courtyard. I could hear mumbling, as if from many voices, and occasionally, soft weeping.

"Many people are praying for... well you know, they are praying," whispered Alphonso.

At the top of the hill, we turned and crossed the street into the parking garage beneath the Pavilion. At the entrance, we were stopped by a smiling guard.

"He jes' arrived," explained Alphonso with his thumb. "They found him in Riverside this morning."

The guard smiled and shook my hand.

"Glad to meet you, sir. We just have some paperwork to fill out and we'll get you into an apartment for the week. This way."

I said goodbye to Alphonso and thanked him. He smiled and I hoped I might meet him again, if just to buy him dinner, but more because I liked his quiet company.

So here I am, in my "apartment". I have a sleeping bag, toiletries in a plastic sack, some snack bars, and an appointment for the showers in the morning. The guard walked me down through eight brightly illuminated levels and back into the depths of the garage. Finally, he found my "apartment" and unlocked the sliding door to a sixties-era apple-red Volkswagen van.

"It's quiet time right now, so if you have any music, headphones please. Enjoy your stay," said the guard. Or the property manager.

So, I have one week, courtesy of the New California Republic, to stay here in the van-partment. After that, I have to show work and residence or be listed as a vagrant, in which case I'll be assigned to a work camp or a mental health facility. At least that's what the paperwork said. Once I was in my sleeping bag and staring at the roof, I thought I'd fall right to sleep. But I didn't. Now after writing all this, I'm starting to feel like I could sleep.

It's nice here.

November 22nd

Who am I kidding?

There're not that many people left.

In the showers the attendants were talking to me, glibly, about how many people had survived.

It's not a very high number.

After the showers, I was so depressed I came back here to my van-partment and crawled into my sleeping bag. I slept badly for an hour.

Who am I kidding? The odds of Alex being alive are thin.

And yet, I am alive.

November 23rd

I am cold and tired. I've been sitting up in the plaza above my van-partment, talking with this kid for hours. Listening, really. I don't know what to think, so I'm going to write down my whole day and read it tomorrow. Maybe I'm just tired and not crazy.

Here goes.

I slept through yesterday. I woke up at night and ate a snack bar and drank some water. Then I just lay on my sleeping bag and watched the roof of the van. I think I drifted off sometime after two.

This morning when I woke up, I went up to the garage entrance and walked out into a bright blue Southern California morning. There were people on the streets. Not a lot, but some.

The same smiling guard came up to me.

"How do you feel?" he asked.

"Honestly?" I said, and he nodded.

"I don't know. I don't feel."

He took off his cap and wiped the sweat from his forehead.

"Downhill from here, off in that direction," He pointed. "you'll find most people. There are some job boards at the major intersection if you're interested." Then he smiled again.

I headed off toward the action.

If I was worried that somehow civilization had failed, I didn't need to. In the space of four blocks by four blocks, past barriers erected at the entrances to the major streets, I found civilization again.

Heavily armed guards watched from corner windows as people thronged in and out of open doors, carrying and pushing all kinds of junk.

I passed a van parked on a side street with white lettering written on the side. "Get a Massage from a TV Star". There was a picture of some actress, a headshot, taped to the side of the van. I recognized the picture, but couldn't remember what show she'd been in. When I passed the passenger door of the van, I could see the woman who had once looked like the girl in the headshot. Her face was drawn and tight, her mean mouth turned hard as she dragged on a cigarette angrily. When she saw me, she turned and smiled, showing me the black eye on the other side of her face.

I don't know if I smiled back.

I walked on as people pushed past me with their handfuls and shopping carts full of junk. I smelled cooked meat coming from somewhere, but I never found it. In the windows of the stores, I could see piles of random articles with hand printed signs that gave an amount, always followed by the symbol for CalDollars.

"That's a nice diamond bracelet," said a voice at my shoulder as I stared into one window. I hadn't seen the bracelet, and in truth I hadn't been looking at any one item in particular. I was just trying to wrap my MBA brain around the local economy.

I turned to a portly Middle Eastern man in a loose cotton shirt and dark slacks, his hair trimmed on the sides and bald on top.

"Yeah," I said, locking in on the price. "And twenty-five Cal-Dollars seems… reasonable?"

"Probably," he said without any conviction. "To be honest, I have no idea. What's a CalDollar worth? It's worth what it buys, my friend. It is worth what it buys."

I looked at him.

"I don't mean to be vague," he apologized. "I'm saying that a dollar, any dollar, is worth what it will buy. You don't understand?" He looked at me for a long moment to see if I understood.

"To put it another way, CalDollars are worth far more today than they might be tomorrow. But who knows? Neither I, nor you. But I can tell you this," he raised one long finger. "They are worth far more than a real diamond bracelet today. Walk with me. I know where we can get some excellent coffee. Do you like coffee?"

We began to walk.

"You see my new friend, what does one do with a real diamond bracelet when the world, or what has become of the world, comes banging on the plywood you have tacked up over your windows and doors to protect your loved ones?"

We passed into an old shopping arcade complete with overhanging gargoyles and scrollwork running up the sides of the building. The kind of building where some old time Hollywood private eye would have had his detective agency.

The Hanson Building.

We entered a long shadowy arcade of kiosks and shouting.

He stopped speaking until we emerged into a courtyard speckled with oddly mismatched tables and chairs. I could hear the quick peeps and chirps of birds bouncing off the high walls above. He held up a long finger plus another, and waved them at a man in a white apron standing behind a coffee cart. When we were seated at a wrought iron table, he continued.

"Today, the diamond bracelet is worth very little. Far less than the twenty-five my friend in the store was trying to gouge you for. But tomorrow when the world is a different place, it may be worth much more. No, today's diamond bracelet is a forty-four magnum. Now, if that had been in the window, the price would have been almost beyond asking. Today's diamonds are guns. And after that comes medicine, and then food. Clothing even, is expensive. Imagine the mark-up now. There are no mills churning out next year's jacket, so what will we wear when winter begins again? Maybe not the most important question here in Southern California, but what about the rest of the country? No one knows. Who has been there? Have you? No my friend, no one knows what tomorrow will bring. So, today you can get a diamond bracelet for just that much or possibly cheaper, but only if you have money, and I'm not saying you don't, but if you do, you could have a very nice twenty-two target pistol. I know the place and the man. Ammunition not included. Is that what you're looking for?"

The coffee arrived and I drank.

I said, "I have been there."

"Excuse me, my friend?" he said, after sipping his coffee.

"I know what's there. Out there, in the world. I've just come from there."

He paused mid sip, and after a long moment of just holding the cup, finally put down his coffee.

"That is very interesting, my friend. Information is worth much more than a diamond bracelet. You see, the government, this New California, as they call it, they don't know, or they do know and they aren't saying. So what is out there and how do you know?"

I sipped my small coffee. Trading and negotiating. Finally, a skill I knew, and could use.

"I'll tell you what. Teach me what's going on here. Tell me how this economy works and I'll tell you what's going on out there. Deal?"

He thought about my offer.

"How do you know?"

"I left New York ten days ago. I travelled by train through Atlanta, New Orleans, San Antonio, and Tucson."

"Where is the train then, if you came by this manner?"

"Derailed in Riverside."

"Alright then, if you are lying, what was the cost to me? A coffee, not so much. Perhaps another coffee, still not so much. The cost is very little if you are lying."

"I'm not lying."

"Alright, my friend. It was wrong of me to put it in such a blunt manner. Hwang!" He raised two more fingers to the man with the apron. "And a pastry for my friend."

"Alright," he began. "It's very simple. The government, the council that is, has only reclaimed certain portions of the city. Those portions must first undergo Reconstruction. Then we, all these people with their armloads of treasure, can enter and salvage the areas that are open. But not until Reconstruction is complete. All these goods, these diamond bracelets and forty-four magnums, and even a grenade I've heard of, they come here to be exchanged and sold. There are many angles to this business. But

I am only concerned with one. Do you know what the one angle
I am concerned with is?"

The pastry and coffees arrived.

I shook my head indicating I did not.

"Gold."

We sipped our coffee.

"Makes sense," I said. "Gold is a good bet and has been for
most of history. You're betting gold will come back once civilization restarts. Right now everyone wants guns and ammo, and I'm
sure there's a certain segment that still thinks big-screen TVs are
valuable. But you know once the danger passes, gold will be back.
I'm guessing right now it's very cheap."

"Very cheap," he broke in, raising a thick finger. "What can
you do with it at night? Can you eat it? Will it keep you warm?
It's heavy and you can't carry it around. You can't start your car
with it, and that doesn't matter because no one is allowed to drive
unless they work for the government. Also, only one freeway is
open and that, not so much, and if rumors are to be believed,
not all the time. So today, what good is gold, and if you happen to have some I would be very happy to purchase it from you.
Right now, everyone is afraid of the dead. But how many of them
are left? I'm saying, not many. Once they're all gone, diamond
bracelets and gold will be very valuable again, my friend. Very
shortly, things are going to change back to the way they once
were."

I drained my coffee and stood up.

He shot me a sudden, angry look.

"So, what have I purchased?" he said.

I noticed the "my friend" was gone.

"You know that forty-four magnum?"

He said nothing.

"I'd buy it if I were you." Then I turned and walked back through the shopping arcade.

I heard his chair scrape behind me.

"You mean to say it's still that bad out there?"

I turned.

I nodded.

I left.

In the shopping arcade among the crowd, I turned to look at him once more. He was sitting again, his large hands hanging loosely between his knees. He looked sadder than anyone I'd ever seen.

It was late afternoon by the time I made it back up the hill. A nice breeze was blowing, so I took the marble steps up to the top of the plaza. The steps were spattered with rust-colored stains. One man, really a teenager, sat at the top, smoking. I climbed the steps and felt tired. As I neared the top, the kid looked at me and then flicked his cigarette ash onto the step below.

"You wanna smoke?" he asked.

I accepted and sat next to him. Across the street, an avenue of fresh, brown earth led off down the hill. Government buildings, long and squat, were the side-walls of a gash in the earth. The buildings were riddled with bullet holes and shell craters.

"Must have been some fight," I said, dragging on the cigarette.

After a pause, the kid sighed and said, "Sure was."

We smoked in silence.

The afternoon turned orange. To the south, I could see several small columns of black smoke.

"You see that step," he said, pointing to one three below where we sat.

I said I did.

"That step there is the high water mark."

I took a drag and asked, "How so?"

"That's where humanity almost went over the hill and into history. I was a gunner, set up right there in that planter off to the left. We dug it out and made a pit for the gun. I'd been fighting with the National Guard for three weeks when we came into L.A. I'm from up around Shasta. Joined the Guard after high school. Anyway, we heard there were still survivors here in these buildings. We set up a heliport on top of that pile of rubble behind us when it was still a building."

I turned and looked back across the plaza. Piles of concrete and rebar reached into the orange sky where there must have once stood an office building.

"We set up a base and started pulling ops into the buildings all over downtown. We heard there was a big group of dead coming up out of Orange County. Anyway, our commander wanted to pull out, but the Lady wouldn't let him. She told him we could kill all of 'em right down there in a trap she and her crew were leadin' 'em into." He pointed to the scraped brown earth where a few bulldozers were parked.

"And we did. We killed 'em all right there in what used to be a big old park. That step was how far they got. Three more and they would have punched through our line. We'd be finished now. Look! I was forward down there in that pit. They came screaming up through where City Hall used to be, we blew that up, and then we all started shooting from these buildings. Even got an airstrike in on 'em. In the end, I was firing point blank with a fifty and they still kept coming. My buddy was tossing grenades as fast as he could pull the pin, and they still kept coming. People were startin' to drop their weapons and run for the heliport. That's when she blew up the building behind us. She didn't want us using it to escape. She and her crew found some C-4 and blew it to high heaven. Then we knew we had to fight. Then it was on. Know what I mean?"

I didn't say anything.

"She was smart. Smarter than our CO who did nothing but get guys killed for three weeks. Then she comes through here like a bat out of hell, and every one of 'em is chasing her right into our kill zone. Still, it wasn't easy. For a good hour there, I thought I was a goner. For a good hour, I thought I was next."

He lit us each another cigarette.

"I can't hardly get over that, you know. I can't let that day go. And I know I've got to. I've got to go on living now. Got to, but I can't."

We sat in silence, smoking. He was generous with his cigarettes.

I knew now what was under all that scraped brown earth.

The numbers.

The numbers were under the earth.

"Debbie Harry with a shotgun," mumbled the kid, as the last of the day faded into evening dark.

I almost couldn't believe what he'd just said.

"What did you just say?" I asked him.

He looked at me.

"Jes' Debbie Harry. Debbie Harry with a shotgun. I didn't mean to disrespect her. Really. Do you know her?"

"Who?"

"The Lady."

"Why'd you call her Debbie Harry with a shotgun?"

"She carried a big ol' shotgun. Right here at the top of the steps. She had it slung across her back when she jumped out of that high-end hummer with the machine gun on top. The car's beat to hell and smoking, and she jumps out and hops the barricade. There were already thousands of 'em rushing through the kill-zone, and there must have been three-hundred of us throwing everything we had right at 'em. She slings that shotgun around and starts pumping blasts into the dead, point-blank. Held 'em right there at that third step. If they'd crossed those three steps, I'm sure she wouldn't have moved. She knew it was all or nothing right there. Hell of a lady."

"No. Why'd you call her Debbie Harry?"

"Oh. She looked like the chick from that eighties band. Real cute."

And that's the way it happened.

I don't want to think about it.

I want to sleep.

It's almost too much to believe.

The Lady.

Debbie Harry.

Alex.

November 24th

I've asked around, and no one seems to know where I can find this "Lady". It's just after three in the morning.

I'm leaving. I've been lying here awake all night, trying to figure out what to do next. Which is really a lie. I know what to do.

Go south, find that hotel, and start looking for Alex. If it's a dead end…

If I don't find her there, then I'll pursue this "Lady". But first, I've got to get clear on what I know. What is known. What can be known? I know Alex was at that hotel the day it all went down.

I couldn't stay in my sleeping bag inside the Van-Partment a minute longer. I had to get up. At first it was just to slide open the door of the bus and get some air. Then it was to stand. I smoked and then I started writing. I heard someone snoring a few "apartments" away. I started packing, and just as I was about to leave, I heard someone, a woman I think, start screaming, "Get them off me! Get them off me!" She screamed the same words over and over. Then she was sobbing and I could hear someone comforting her. Murmuring to her.

I picked up the Big Bertha and laid it across my shoulder.

I thought, "I'm leaving now."

It's four o'clock in the afternoon. I've been walking all day, and I've just crossed into some rail yards south of the city.

I passed a man selling street tacos and asked how much. I didn't have any money. No CalDollars. The tacos smelled great. I traded my military canteen for two of them and a warm beer. The tacos were spicy and the beer made them even spicier. My mouth was burning. I sat there wondering if it had been a stupid idea to trade my canteen.

Beyond the rail yard is the Southern Wall.

That's what everybody calls it. The Southern Wall. Supposedly, I can slip through and move into the abandoned neighborhoods beyond. From what I understand, those neighborhoods have been cleared, but are not yet open to salvage. Meaning, no one can go in and loot them. The main looting activity is concerned with the West Side of Los Angeles. The Board of Directors, the local governing authority, wants a clear path of retreat to the ocean in case anything comes out of the desert.

It's almost dusk and soon it will be winter, but the days are still warm and even hot at times. It seems like it hasn't rained in forever. Everything is covered in ash and fine dust. The sky is a hazy orange.

November 25th

I spent the night at a freeway guard post south of Los Angeles. I tried to slip through the wall and into the neighborhoods yesterday evening, but it's pretty heavily guarded with lots of people walking a makeshift wall of stacked and smashed cars topped with plywood walkways and search lights.

When I told them I needed to get down to Newport Beach, they told me the only way to get there was by the Five freeway in one of the twice-daily buses that's allowed to use the recently cleared highway.

I walked east along the rail yard toward the freeway. The rail yard is brightly lit and there's lots of activity as bulk goods are being moved in and offloaded from large trucks. The local militia seems to be setting up some kind of fort here, and I was asked repeatedly if I was looking for a specific unit to join. I said little and kept moving. I reached the highway in the evening.

A heavily armed sniper team led by a woman named Marie told me I couldn't get onto the freeway until 6 a.m. the next morning. They let me sleep in a circle of light outside their post. They said little and kept the radio low throughout the night. Several times I awoke to whispering talk. I wondered what time it was and every time I checked, it wasn't even close to six. It was cold and I slept badly.

In the foggy morning light, I smelled burnt ash, and one of the guards talked about a fire he'd seen in the night out beyond the Southern Wall, somewhere in the seemingly endless sprawl of neighborhoods. It'd burned for a few hours, then gone out.

"Probably just another burn pile down in Compton," said Marie.

I asked where I could catch the bus and they said usually right there. But the bus was cancelled for the day. After a few calls on a landline, they opened up the gate leading down onto the freeway and told us, me and the others who had arrived, that we could walk the freeway to the next checkpoint today. No one else wanted to go even though they told us not to worry; apparently there were sniper teams on every overpass.

And there were. Every overpass had a small team of militia. The streets leading onto the overpasses were blocked off with cars and big rigs, and the bridges themselves were fortified with barbed wire and large guns. Machine guns I guess. On every bridge, I saw two people with telescopes or binoculars scanning down into the urban sprawls off to the sides of the freeway.

Around ten, a man on a horse passed by at a trot. He nodded, touching his cowboy hat, then kicked his horse into a slow gallop, and I lost sight of him as the road curved ahead.

At three, I came upon a crew clearing the side of the road of overgrown grass and trees. They burned great piles of brown palm fronds and dry grass, vegetation that had grown unchecked for the last three months. I asked if they had any water, and they gave me a small bottle and returned to their work. I drained the bottle and wondered if I actually might die of thirst.

It was stupid of me to have traded the canteen.

I've got to realize the world has changed.

It's night now, and I'm sleeping beneath a guarded overpass. The soldiers lit two fire barrels off to each side, but they won't let me come up onto the bridge. So I'm sleeping in the median below the bridge near the barrels.

I need stuff if I'm going to find Alex.

November 26th

I couldn't take it a minute longer. The guys on top of the bridge were obnoxious. For the first half of the night, it sounded like they were getting drunk. They were playing cards, and every time someone won a hand, they would yell or curse. One guy in particular would slap his hand on the plywood boards they were playing on and yell, "That's how it's done!" Every time. He won a lot and never changed up his catch phrase. Later, two of them began to take pot shots into the surrounding neighborhood, cackling each time they hit something.

Their leader, a whiny-voiced man, finally shut them up and sent them to bed.

I picked up my stuff quietly and climbed the side of the hill under the bridge. I found a hole in the fence and crawled through it. It was time to get off the beaten path. Maybe I could find some stuff, or at least some water.

Now I was in the neighborhoods.

I inched along a wall covered in graffiti near the main road that led away from the bridge, and climbed over it once I got near the road. I was in someone's backyard again staring at the back of a house.

The house looked decrepit and overrun. I had to find something to use. I had to find tools I would need to survive. Tools I would use to find Alex.

I entered through an open screen door on the porch. Inside, mattresses were thrown across what had once been a family room. I could see empty bottles on the floor in the pale light coming from the guard towers on the overpass. There was little left in the house except a painting someone had slashed to pieces. The upstairs was a pile of scattered clothing thrown onto the floor. Drawers were flung open, and whatever useful thing had been found and taken. I went downstairs and into the garage. I found nothing more than rusting garden tools.

For a moment, I stood in the musty smelling garage feeling completely frustrated.

I was heading off the beaten path now. I needed to find things I could use, and in the first house I'd searched, there had been nothing worth taking. Still, I felt I had to take something. But I'm not kidding, everything I looked at felt totally useless to me in regards to any obstacle I could conceive of facing in the near-term future.

I left the house feeling dejected as I cut across the unkempt dead lawn. I could go back and stick to the freeway, but that felt hopeless. What would I find along its sides that could help me? The truth was, I was hungry and needed water.

The searchlight from the bridge lazily swept over the neighborhoods on the other side of the freeway.

I cut diagonally away from the bridge, passing through a neighborhood of single-story ranchero-style houses. All of them had once been painted different colors, but now in the pale light of night, they seemed a single disheartening gray. Every window was smashed, doors had been torn from their hinges, clothing and kitchen utensils lay scattered from front doorways across short lawns, ending their trails in the leaf-glutted gutters. The few cars that remained were missing tires. In their smashed windows, I saw an abundance of wires and missing radios.

I felt like I'd gone about a mile more when I found the business avenue heading west. Here I found more stores smashed and looted. There had been no defense. No boarded windows or burn piles in the streets. None of those things. Here, there had just been looting and chaos. And now it was all gone and I wondered what had become of the looters, who in those first days of lawlessness and disorder had found some kind of unlimited shopping paradise. I eventually had to walk in the street to avoid all the broken glass that lay in thick piles across the sidewalk.

Then the neighborhood changed. The businesses here had long ceased holding forth. Long before the outbreak. Here, were large corporate "for sale" signs smashed to pieces behind chain link fences, and gas stations where the pumps had disappeared long ago. Vacant car lots that hadn't see a new model in years, remained long after the fluttering multicolored flags and EZ Credit signs had disappeared. All that remained were the faded white-washed words "Out of Business".

For some, the apocalypse had taken place long before that hot day back in August.

In the hours before dawn, as I walked and talked myself out of searching buildings that looked dark and friendless, I thought about what I had done and aspired to be before the end of the world. I had worked on Wall Street. I'd been a broker. I wasn't about to get all sappy and wonder how many of my decisions had influenced these streets. But still, I wondered about these streets where my decisions had come to rest, and what they looked like now as opposed to then, on those optimistic days of the past when all these vacant lots and boarded up buildings had offered "EZ Credit". Did all the streets of the world somehow bear the weight of my decisions and resemble this present wasteland?

Was this my hell?

Was this my punishment?

At dawn, lost in thought, I barely heard the scraping sound that had been following me for some time.

He was black. The only part of his body that moved like a human was the right leg that seemed to jut out in front of his body. The rest followed the leg, as if tethered to it. His head was cranked to the side and his mouth, a red gash that contrasted his ashy blackness, hung agape as if on the verge of objecting to my presence.

I watched him come for me.

The streets were turning morning blue, and by the time he was within ten feet of me, the tops of the buildings had turned to gold. I could hear birds.

I was done with running.

I was done with climbing further and further up the Tower.

I was done living in fear.

I was hungry.

I was tired.

I was thirsty.

I was done.

I hit him with the Big Bertha.

In the second before I struck him, I felt all the rage of the past three months boil up within me. But that wasn't enough to hit him in the head, the place where Carmichael used to crush them with his Derek Jeter Monday Morning Meeting Bat.

Signed and everything.

It wasn't enough.

I hesitated as I raised the Big Bertha over my shoulder.

I knew what it would sound like, and I felt the power the fancy club would transfer directly into the side of his head.

And it wasn't enough to do it.

In some way, he was still like me.

And in some way, he and those like him, through no fault of their own, had killed everyone I'd ever loved.

I thought about Alex.

That was enough to do it.

Except the Big Bertha wasn't up to it.

It shattered, breaking into fiberglass shards as it dislocated the dead-thing's jaw crookedly to one side.

He reached necrotic arms out for me as I stumbled backward from the impact.

I truly hadn't expected that.

I thought I'd be dealing with the effects of what I had done to the corpse. Dealing with the anger and guilt and yes, even shame, as I considered the now permanently dead thing lying at my feet.

But it was not lying dead at my feet.

Instead, it lunged forward, snarling through its broken jaw while milky eyes rolled upward in their sockets.

I ran.

I could hear it galloping after me saying, "Go to your left, go to your left."

I stumbled, feeling the energy drain from my legs all at once.

I heard a single gunshot as I weaved to my left, running back onto the sidewalk, tripping and then slamming into a morning-shadowed wall that still held the cold of night as my hands pushed off it. I could hear my ragged breathing against the face of the wall in the moment I connected with it.

"Stop! I got 'em."

When I turned, the cowboy from yesterday was dismounting his horse with his rifle in hand. He walked forward toward the fallen corpse of the black man. He stood over the body for a moment. Then he walked, business-like, back to the horse and dropped his rifle into a holster hanging from the side of the saddle. He returned with a small hatchet and bent down over the corpse.

I watched in horror as he pulled a neckerchief up around his nose and mouth.

"Close your mouth and eyes and don't breathe for a second."

But I didn't close my eyes.

He swung the hatchet down on its neck, severing the head.

The spray, there was little, went off to one side.

"They don't have too much left in 'em now. Not if they've been this way for a while. But it pays to be safe," said the cowboy.

He went back to his horse and retrieved a large pair of pliers and a canvas sack. He gripped the head with the pliers and deposited it into the sack.

"Come help me burn the body, then we'll have breakfast in a park up the way. Name's Chris. Yours?"

He didn't need my help as I watched him burn the headless corpse.

I'm writing this now, sitting at a picnic table in a city park.

Chris is making our breakfast, coffee and oatmeal over a barbecue pit. The horse is grazing in the dead grass.

November 27th

We are somewhere east of the 405 freeway.

We crossed over the 710 freeway on a small bridge. Below the bridge, a sea of cars trailed off in both directions, residents of a never-ending traffic jam. We are heading into northern Long Beach near the old Boeing factory. Apparently there's a hangar with some of the infected still trapped inside.

That's what Chris does. He's a bounty hunter for the Directorate. He collects infected heads for fifty CalDollars a pop.

According to Chris, as related at the picnic table in the city park yesterday over oatmeal and pretty good black coffee, most of Southern California's urban sprawl has been declared safe. That is, clear of the infected. I guess the big battle at City Center the kid on the steps told me about, was the culmination of a plan to draw all of them into one kill zone, and that went a long way toward solving everybody's walking corpse problem. Kind of like the Holland Tunnel. All that remains now are infected that didn't take the bait either because they can't, i.e. they're stuck in a warehouse, or because they simply didn't bite the "follow the leader" plan that lead to the burn piles and mass graves at City Center. Now the corpses that remain are more just a nuisance to salvagers once the area has been Reconstructed.

Some nuisance.

Bounty hunters, in with the local government, contract to go out and clean up the infected, bringing back their heads as proof. The government does this so groups of salvagers don't go out, get bit, and turn into a typhoon of infected. It also explains why areas are off limits until they've been deemed safe and then undergone the process of Reconstruction, which I'm not sure I wholly understand yet.

"That's fifty CalDollars per head. You already got twenty-five from the gentleman in the sack. You want to make a few dollars more?" asked Chris.

We sat eating steaming oatmeal in the morning sunlight. The picnic table beneath our hands was carved on every available surface with gang affiliations, pledges of love, and other unreadable words.

"Course I'll pay you once we reach the Huntington Beach Outpost. But between here and there, I've got to check this hangar they say has a few of 'em still hanging around inside. I guess someone locked 'em up in it and they can't get out. If you help me, you'll have some money when we reach Huntington Beach."

I thought about my shattered Big Bertha and wondered how much help I'd actually be.

"I was just a stockbroker."

He took a sip from his coffee and seemed to consider the sky.

"I'm an actor," he replied. "I mean, I was an actor before everything went haywire. But I wasn't always an actor. I have a degree in engineering. I used to work on robots out at JPL."

The sun grew warm as we sat there. I felt tired, but in another way, alive, almost electric.

"I always wanted to be an actor," Chris continued. "One day I decided I'd lived enough of other people's dreams, and I might try something else for a space. So, I decided I'd try acting."

"You look like a cowboy," I said.

"I love horses. If that makes me a cowboy, then I guess I am one. I've played a lot of them in Japanese beer commercials and a few of the new westerns."

When it was time to leave, we walked, him leading the horse, casting a wary eye into the side streets we passed, me trailing alongside, listening for something I now knew to listen for. That sandy shuffle-scrape they make. When Chris talked, which was seldom, it was to let me know what he was doing or what we needed to consider as we crossed the quiet remains of Compton.

"Watch the windows for movement. They could still be in there."

And...

"The street up ahead is wide. If we see one there, might be more nearby. They'll all come out at once, so be ready to move."

And...

"When all this started, I saddled Chief and we just rode up into the San Gabriels. Spent three weeks up there, pretty much alone, though not always."

And...

"Chief's an old movie horse I got for cheap. He's good, little mean sometimes. He'll bite ya, so watch out."

And...

"One day it's gonna rain again and wash all this away."

When we crossed over the 710, we entered newer neighborhoods, long stretches of tract housing not so economically blighted before everything happened. The damage here almost seemed worse though. The smell of past fires came long before we entered vast swathes of burned-out buildings. Whole streets had caught fire. Even light posts had burned. In the ruins of a strip mall, near the hollow shell of a supermarket, we found a fluttering yellow marker. We walked Chief across the melted asphalt and onto the burnt sidewalk. Next to the fluttering yellow tape, a piece of cardboard was duct-taped to a heat-twisted metal beam.

SURVIVORS HERE

BIGSAV SUPERSTORE

RADIO CONTACT ON OCT 3RD.

26 MEN, 15 WOMEN. UNKNOWN CHILDREN.

LAST CONTACT, OCT 17TH

DATE OF FIRE, UNKNOWN

NO SURVIORS FOUND ON 14 NOVEMBER.

SGT M. GATES, NEW CALIFORNIA REPUBLIC

I stood reading the sign as the breeze moved it ever so slightly. Chris peered over the low brick wall at what remained of the BigSav Super Store.

A square of ashy rubble lay within.

"Must have burned real hot. Chemical fire most likely," said Chris. Then, as if summing up all the wrongs that had conspired against the people listed simply as SURVIVORS, he said, "Reconstruction's gonna have a hell of a time with this bunch."

A small breeze began to stir the ashes inside the wreckage.

"I don't think anyone'll ever rebuild this. I mean, that's not the plan, is it? Rebuild everything as it was, is that what Reconstruction means?"

"I don't think there is a plan, Jase."

He calls me "Jase".

"No, Reconstruction's this idea the Board of Governors has. In essence, they're going to find out what happened to everyone, as much as they can, and identify as many remains, both infected and survivors, as it is possible to do. That's what Reconstruction means. A Reconstruction of events for the permanent record. Until an area has been "Reconstructed", no one can salvage there, loot really, until everything's been cleared by the Department for both Infected and Reconstruction."

We watched the breeze stir the ash, and in our way, I knew each of us was trying to conduct our own Reconstruction of what had happened within that square of ash. Of what had happened to these people who would now only be known as "survivors".

Even though they hadn't.

Tonight we can see the big hangars of the Boeing aircraft plant and the wide stretches of concrete that lead to the runway. We are camped in the pool area of an old apartment complex called The Kona Breeze.

Chris picked the locked gate to get us into the pool area.

"It's a skill I learned for a "B" movie about carjacking," he muttered, while working the lock with a small set of tools he kept in his back pocket. Once inside, he led the horse through and tethered him to some small yellowing palms.

"We'll be safer in here for the night. There still might be some of them around, and with this high pool fence, I doubt they'll get through."

Then he checked the pool.

It was empty.

"Well, that's good. For us, that is."

"How so?"

"We can sleep in the empty pool tonight. Move some of these beach chairs down in there and it'll be nice. We can even have a fire. They won't see it because the firelight will be down below the lip of the pool. Still, they might smell the smoke. I don't even know if they can smell, but they might."

He crossed to the restrooms and was gone for a moment.

"Clear in both," he said, as he walked out holstering a large iron-gray revolver.

Then, "We'll have to find some water for Chief."

We went collecting water out of dark refrigerators we found in apartments. Chris pulled the cement cover off water meters in the ground and with a heave, sent them through the windows of the apartments. We did this about five times until we had enough bottled water for Chief.

"Though it weren't all Chief might want," commented Chris.

All the apartments seemed expectantly ordinary, each apartment quietly waiting for their owners to come home as I had supposed, all those weeks in the Tower, my condo might be waiting for me.

Maybe all the apartment residents had worked at the nearby Boeing plant where Chris expected to find future bounties, shambling through the dusty shadows of large buildings they could not find their way out of.

One apartment was completely wrecked as though a savage fight had taken place across its entry hall, living room, kitchenette, bedroom, and bath vanity. A series of bloody handprints seemed to indicate someone had dragged themselves up the stairs to a loft. Chris drew his gun and climbed the stairs cautiously. After a moment he came down.

"She's been gone for a while now," he said quietly.

Back at the pool, we made a fire out of some broken up wood from a flimsy garden trellis we'd passed. Chris heated cans of chili we'd taken from an apartment.

"There's a bag of Doritos, unopened. It'll be nice if we crush 'em on top of the chili and add hot sauce. What do you think, Jase?"

I thought it would be good.

It was.

The meal put some nice warmth in our stomachs, and for a long time, we watched the fire crackle and throw shadows against the pale blue walls of the empty pool. The night was cold, and soon our breath came forth in puffs of vapor. We pulled our deck chairs closer to the fire and watched the night sky. It looked like a fleet of burning shards drifting over the black depths of a sea I could not comprehend the bottom of.

I realize now that I have wasted large portions of my life on things that hold little value in light of what has happened to us.

In the night, I awoke and the fire was nothing but the smell of ash. I could hear something banging into the pool gate above us. There was a soft moan each time it bounced off the gate. Chief seemed a little bothered, doing that thing horses do when they move their feet and begin to let you know they don't like something. It was full dark and the moon had gone down. I could see the dim outline of the thing at the far end of the pool behind the silhouette of the gate.

"It's one of 'em," I heard Chris whisper. "He's been there for a while. I'm just waiting to see if more show up."

We watched it bang into the gate once more with a sickly "huff".

"Alright," said Chris, and his revolver suddenly roared in a flash of bright fire and a sharp crack that echoed off the walls of the apartments surrounding us.

The thing fell over.

"I was aiming for the throat. Blow the head off so we could turn him in."

I heard Chris turn over in his sleeping bag.

"But I might've got him in the head," he mumbled. "We'll find out in the morning."

A few minutes later I could hear Chris sleeping again.

November 28ᵗʰ

This morning, we found that our midnight caller was once Josh Meyers according to his driver's license. His pockets were stiff with cash and watches.

"Must have survived for a few days of looting," Chris mumbled as he turned out the corpse's pockets.

Josh's head was mostly intact besides the bullet hole in his nose. But when Chris picked up the head after severing it with the hatchet, we found that the back of the skull had been blown wide open.

"Still good," Chris said and dropped it into his canvas sack. "That's another twenty-five for you, Jase."

We walked Chief out onto an overgrown football field near the hangars and let him graze. Chris took his rifle and binoculars, and we climbed through a downed fence onto the edge of a giant aircraft runway.

"Contract says that big yellow hangar over there is where

they're at. A scout picked 'em out two weeks ago. So who knows if they're still in there?"

"How many?" It's always the numbers with me.

"Couldn't say with any accuracy, Jase, but he thought maybe five. Problem is, looters might have come in and got more than they bargained for. So, there could be more in there now."

We crossed onto the wide apron of the runway.

"But that was all from the contract boss. So maybe we should expect more. There was a reason no one wanted this job, other than it being two weeks old and a bit of a trek. So I guess we'd better plan on more. You know how to shoot?"

I was staring at the wreckage of a large aircraft that had crashed at the far end of the runway.

"That's something, huh?" said Chris. "Saw it last time I came through here. One of them big airliners. Must have been a hell of a day."

"No, I can't shoot," I said. "I mean, I've never shot a gun in my life. So I don't know if I can or can't."

"Well, now's not the time to learn."

We crossed into the shadow of a hangar which rose maybe five stories above us.

I picked up a rusty metal pipe I found lying on the tarmac.

It was the most thrilling day of my life.

Pretty sick, huh?

The hangar had a big padlock on a small side door. Chris shot it off and pulled the door open. Inside, through thick yellow shafts of light and dusty brown shadows, we could see the diseased dead milling about. There were maybe fifty of them.

Now it's almost eleven o'clock at night and we're still burning headless corpses in the middle of the runway. We're going to sleep on top of the wrecked aircraft tonight.

If we sleep at all.

Chris just came back in from circling the dead grass at the side of the runway.

"That's over two-hundred." Meaning he'd just found another corpse out there in the night, lying in the tall grass. Waiting to have its head cut off and exchanged for payment.

"Too many of them," Chris had said the moment after we'd opened the door to the hangar. "Fall back!"

I ran for the center of the runway as they came flooding out of the hangar. Chris was already working his lever-action rifle, but for every one of them he dropped, two pushed their gray-green arms out the narrow door.

"Gotta reload, keep moving away from them," he shouted to me over his shoulder. I watched him trot back across the concrete apron as he threw his rifle across his broad shoulders and drew his revolver, dropping two women, scabby and gray, almost screaming as they lunged for his throat. He fired, and after each shot, thumbed the hammer back and fired again, almost point blank into their skulls as they came at him.

"Head for the wreck at the far end of the runway!" he shouted, falling farther behind me.

I did. I felt sick. Sick with fear like back in the Tower. Except, I was out in the open now. Exposed. There was no Tower to climb up. No stairwell doors to barricade. I ran for the massive, sprawling, broken airliner and saw in its cracked fuselage a smiling death grin in the smashed cockpit. It was as if it was telling me of everything that was possible if one of those things should get a hold of me.

I heard two more shots, and watched as Chris ran out from underneath a cloud of blue gun smoke, holstering his pistol. He picked bullets off his belt and fed them into the rifle.

He saw me watching and waved for me to keep moving.

"Get up on top. You'll be safer there."

I didn't look back until I'd climbed onto the wreck, using the wing and then a broken-out window to barely lunge high enough to cling to the fuselage and crawl the rest of the way to the top. When I looked back, Chris was slowly retreating, leaving corpses both thrashing and immobile in his wake.

That's when I saw the others.

In ones and twos, they lurched out across the dry grass surrounding the long runway. They came lumbering out of the neighborhoods and through broken fences, hearing the gun shots and groans, lunging forward as if salvation were somewhere at the end of their eternal fall.

I know that last sentence is a little poetic.

I know whoever reads this might not remember, but I am… was a stockbroker. Words were never my thing. It was the now-meaningless numbers that had meant everything in the life I'd once thought meant something. But since I've been keeping this journal, it feels right when I describe things that way. Written words come easier now that I've been writing more of them. Written words can be beautiful, even when the things you're describing are sometimes horrible.

The way I saw them today. They looked like that.

Like lungers seeking salvation at the end of an eternal fall.

The afternoon was hot, it was midday. I could smell the gun smoke and see sharp puffs of bluish haze that seemed to start at the door we'd opened and follow Chris back across the runway. I could see them, falling and fallen, stumbling forward to meet death.

And it was then, at that very moment, that I felt alive. I could see the difference between them and me. I was still alive.

That was all. One simple fact, and it made all the difference in the world. Their deaths did not diminish me. It made me feel something I had not felt in all these weeks of crossings. It made me feel alive.

For a moment, it was close. We barely got Chris to the top of the wreck. When we did, that's when I learned to shoot. They couldn't get up to us.

Here's how you shoot.

It's just a target.

You don't grip the stock of the rifle.

It rests in your open palm.

The butt goes in the hollow of your shoulder.

One finger pad, just the front of your index finger, rests on the trigger.

You breathe as you aim down the sights.

And just as you exhale…

You squeeze the trigger.

And the target falls down.

It's just a target. Not a human being anymore.

Two-hundred and five was the final total.

Ten-thousand, two-hundred and fifty CalDollars.

November 29th

We had a long walk today.

We left the corpses, piled and burned. Chris packed up all the information we could pull out of their pockets. Of the two hundred and five, maybe half had some kind of identification. Chris bundled it all and we loaded the heads into extra sacks he kept in his saddlebags.

We tied full sacks of heads across Chief who didn't like it, but put up with it. I saw in his horse's eyes that it was yet one more thing he must endure. He snorted and looked away.

Then we each picked up the end of a pole from which we'd tied more hanging sacks of heads, and started out. We crossed northern Long Beach on big east-west streets, cutting through long swathes of more low, ranchero-style houses. There were a lot of car wrecks. Some still had remains lying within the broken glass and shattered plastic. We entered the freeway and walked along the side of it until we came to a jackknifed semi blocking the southbound lanes. The other side of the road was open and clear of cars. Suitcases and lost belongings were strewn haphazardly throughout the lanes, as though people had abandoned their cars and tried to flee, shedding their possessions as they went.

We continued on until we crossed into Seal Beach.

"Huntington Beach Stockade is a few more miles south. From there, I'll try to pick up some more work. I've heard there's some out in the foothills. If you want to come along, we can eventually find you a horse."

I hadn't said much about why I'd been headed to Newport Beach.

"My plan is to find some cattle," continued Chris, as we walked in silence along the empty freeway. He reminded me of someone pitching a stock tip. "If there are any cattle left, then I'll start raising 'em down along the Irvine Coast. Good cattle country in the hills above the ocean. Eventually people are going to want fresh meat and well, I figure I could sell 'em some. If you want to go partners, we could give it a try."

The sun was fading into the west.

I smelled rain.

Before that moment, I'd never smelled rain in my entire life. In fact, I'd never cared if it rained one way or the other. I'd just accepted it. If it was raining when I walked out the front door of my childhood home, prep-school dorm, college apartment, stockbroker condo, then it was raining, and I dealt with it.

I smelled rain.

There wasn't a cloud in the sky.

"Think about it, Jase. You're a good man to have around," he said. Then as he looked up at the sun, "Rain tonight."

We arrived at the Huntington Beach Stockade, just off the freeway. A makeshift wall of buses surrounded a small complex of business offices and a large pizza restaurant.

Or, what had once been all those things.

Now it was the southernmost organized outpost of the New California Republic.

We passed through the gate and Chris found Jackson, the Superintendent of the Stockade.

"I got two-hundred and seven heads," said Chris, including the midnight caller and the guy I'd broken my Big Bertha on.

"Two-hundred and seven," whistled Jackson. "Didn't know there were that many left."

I thought about all those ravening hordes that clutched at the train as we fled west through Atlanta and New Orleans. I thought about the men on the train we'd left behind.

"I don't know about that, but there aren't as many as there were," laughed Chris, untying the sacks from Chief.

"Alright, drop 'em over there. I'll count 'em and find you later with a check."

"Prefer cash."

"Ain't got enough. But I will have, Friday. If you're about, I can pay you then. You know I'm good for it."

"Yeah, guess you'll have to be."

We staked Chief near some trees in the back of the parking lot. I stayed with him while Chris got water and apples.

"Let's drink a bit," he said when he got back.

The pizzeria had once been some corporate chain joint. Now it was filled with liquor bottles and cases of beer. You paid your admission and then you could drink as much as you could find in the cases and boxes on the floor. We were sternly warned by a guy named "Tank" not to abuse the largesse.

When we had our drinks, we sat back in a booth and talked.

"So what is it you've got to do?" asked Chris.

I sipped my warm crown and coke. Chris had a bottle of beer.

"If you don't know if someone's alive," I began, "should you try to find them? Even if there's not much evidence they might still be?"

He thought about my question for a long time and finally, after a sip from his beer, said, "I don't know."

We sat there. A couple of girls came around. One was so drunk she couldn't speak. The other wanted to know if we might like company.

Chris smiled warmly. "I might. But I think my friend has someone he needs to find." Then he looked at me. "Isn't that right, Jase? Isn't that what you meant?"

I nodded. I guess it was.

They left with Chris and I drank my Crown Royale until I was down to half the bottle. Later, someone came in with a violin, and shortly someone else joined with a harmonica.

They played sad songs that were familiar, and yet I could not remember their names.

Except for "Waltzing Matilda".

I knew that one.

An old man began to sing. He'd been there all along with his head down on the bar. Then he sat up from his place and walked over to the players, and began to sing.

It was sad and beautiful all at once.

I'd never heard music like that before. Simple music. A violin, a harmonica, and a not perfect voice. It was a far cry from the clubs and commercial jingles that had once filled my daily music allotments.

I thought about Alex.

There was a chance she could be here. Maybe even someone here, if she'd survived, knew her. Knew of her.

Or maybe she'd gone to New York to find me. As soon as it all began. She had gone to find me like I should have gone to find her. I should've made it out of the office that day and started driving. Driving to find the woman I would marry.

The woman I loved.

Love.

That should be one of my four shames.

But it isn't.

I left the bar with my bottle. The night sky was overcast, and orange lights from the fort's perimeter gave the fog a warm glow. Mist obscured the far end of the street.

A dog barked.

I returned to Chief and rolled out my sleeping bag. Chris had left a little pile of sticks he said we'd keep for our night's fire. I started the fire like he'd taught me the night before.

And now I will write about Carmichael.

Which is the third of my shames.

After Derek is gone, there is just Carmichael and Kathy and me. We are on thirty-nine, I think. It took forever to get through the last ceiling and when we get to this floor, we find it is a modeling agency. We come up through the floor in a main corridor. Everything is quiet. We listen.

Nothing.

And so we're up.

We smell. It's been almost two weeks in the same clothes. The only water we can find is bottled, as the sinks and toilets have long since ceased providing any. But there is abundance here in the modeling agency. Big flats of bottled water lie waiting and stacked in a break room. We've been living off snacks. Granola bars, power bars, trail mix. How much longer until we're rescued?

The floor is devoted almost solely to the modeling agency. Large pictures of vacant-eyed models adorn the wide, white curving hallways that were yesterday's future.

What has become of all these waiflings?

I doubt they had the calories to spare to run from, fight against, and barricade out, the living dead.

There's camera equipment and bottled water. There is even a lot of cocaine. But there is no food. Not even in the kitchen. There's vodka. There's Champagne.

But there is no food.

Outside, present mid-plague New York is the morning after the worst party of all time. I see a building fully engulfed in flames a few blocks away. Down below, the streets are deserted and covered in dust and ash. Abandoned cars jam intersections. The building that we used to wave to the other survivors in, the other us, looks neglected. Sometimes I see a shadow move behind a dusty window over there.

But nothing definite.

Kathy Henderson-Kiel is haranguing Carmichael about food. Carmichael, bat in hand, is clearing every office. His shirt is spattered in dried blood from the countless people he has beaten back to real death. I mean, the infected he has beaten to death again. Is that right?

Today, I hope he doesn't find any.

I need a break from that whole scene.

If you look closely at the bat, you'll see he's carved tick marks.

"Home run!" he whispers, imitating the roar of a crowd every time it's over. "Home run!" His eyes, brown, molasses brown, are vacant.

If you really let go of reality, if you really allow yourself to analyze the situation, you almost believe that he thinks it is a "Home run!" every time he finds one of them on a new floor. Yes, he's doing all the work. He's clearing all the rooms, while you rifle the few desks you find on this level, and part of you hopes for a gun as much as a Snickers bar, and you don't even let yourself think that what you'd really like to find is a nice roast turkey with all the trimmings. No, today you'd just settle for that Snickers bar. Or that gimme a break, gimme a break, break me off a piece of that Kit Kat Bar. Anything, because frankly you are starving.

To death.

Yes, he, Carmichael your best friend, is doing all the work as Kathy Henderson-Kiel shadows him, and you know some nights they sneak away and you can hear them together and yes, you're even jealous because you can't think for a second, looking out at what has become of New York and what must surely be the rest of the world, that there is an Alex left somewhere in this kind of world. Yes, you're thinking, he's doing all the work.

But...

If you have to hear him whisper "Home run!" as he imitates a screaming stadium roar, one more time, you'll lose it. You pray he doesn't find one on this floor. Just this floor. Just this once. Don't let him find one because you know that's what he loves now.

Finding one.

Finding one of them.

And he doesn't.

And for a moment, you're relieved. It's a break.

You deserve a break today.

And when everyone gathers in the main office and Kathy Henderson-Kiel picks up an absurdly groovy desk phone and tries to get a dial tone for the umpteenth time, you close your eyes and grit your teeth because that's almost as bad as "Home run!"

There's coke.

Cocaine.

Whatever that's for, you say as you lay out the other prizes. Snacks, peanuts, and candy you don't find. Instead there's coke, vodka, and water.

And for some reason, your stomach is churning because there is something in that little conversation of items that screams, "Bad idea!"

Later, when things are supposed to be mellow, they're not. They're tense. Things are tense, so Carmichael does more coke.

There's enough coke to do more coke.

In fact, there's enough coke to do a lot of coke.

In fact, there's enough to do too much coke.

How do you know when one of your merry band of survivors has done too much?

"Hey bro. B-R-O," says Carmichael. "I need a little work-out. Whadd'ya say we open the stairwell door and I get in a few practice swings?"

He tightens and loosens his grip on the bat. His knuckles are white. His face is red. His eyes are deep pools.

Bad idea.

"No really, it's good, buddy," he assures me. "Just need to work off some of this coke. Plus, maybe I could clear them out. Maybe we could make it down to the street. Just watch my back and keep the door open. Just a few swings. Gotta keep in shape for the big game, y'know." And then he looks at the ceiling. As though we must go up there. As though the big game still lies ahead.

We only go up to a new floor when the banging on the stairwell doors gets to the point that it sounds like they're, the dead, the walking corpses, the infected, are going to get through fairly soon. Then up we go. It usually takes about a day and a half for that to happen. Then up we go.

Right now it's silent.

One of them, at that very moment, has the bad timing to slap the stairwell door at the end of the hall.

"Come on, baby," says Kathy Henderson-Kiel like some common street whore trying to talk her pimp down off an old-school beat-down. "I'll take care of you." This is a woman who graduated Magna Cum Laude from Harvard. This is a woman who cleared seven figures a year in trades. And now...

"No!" shouts Carmichael. "I need to take a few swings. Just that guy. Just that guy there and I'll be fine."

You realize, at this very moment, that your best friend is a psychotic killer. Less Roland, more Blaine the Mono.

You also realize the word "friend" might not mean so much, what with all the coke lying around.

And the vodka.

And the end of the world outside the windows.

You try to stop him. She tries to stop him. But in the end,

you're pushing open the fire door for him. A startled and very sick corpse on the other side of the door stumbles backward.

Surprised almost.

Carmichael is suddenly on him, swinging and grunting.

"Home run!"

And then…

"Follow me!"

But you don't.

And he disappears down the dark stairwell.

The emergency lights are still on. Everything is bathed in a red, bloody wash.

You hear Carmichael below in the darkness, grunting as he swings.

There are pulpy sounds.

There is groaning.

There is the sound they make. That shuffle moan.

You don't hear "Home run!"

But you know he's saying it. Each time.

"Follow me guys! I'm goin' all the way," he shouts, his voice echoing up the stairwell.

"Home run!"

And then he's in over his head.

He's grunting hard, almost breathlessly.

There's the sound of splintering wood. The sound a bat makes when it shatters. It's almost an understated "crack", sharp and quick, but it speaks volumes for what you can't see down below.

There's not so much swinging and connecting now, down there in the red dark.

"Help!" he says as a matter of fact.

Surprised almost.

And Kathy Henderson-Kiel is screaming his name from the landing in the stairwell.

Carmichael is also screaming when you close the fire door behind yourself and Kathy Henderson-Kiel.

Home run!

Shame.

Feeling, as you lay down that night on couches no sane person would ever buy, and over which models once draped or threw themselves across as they sold blouses, watches, and success, along with the illusion of power and the lie of acquisition equaling some nebulous happiness, feeling relieved that you'll never, ever, have to hear "Home run!" again.

That is my third shame.

November 30th

When I woke I could hear the sound of rain, gentle drops, falling intermittently on canvas. In the night, Chris had returned and stretched a tarp between the trees above. There was a smoky fire curling up into the cold morning air.

There was coffee.

Chris sat watching the fire. He was older than I'd thought. He'd seemed about thirty-five. Dark haired, chiseled jaw, the bombardier blue eyes of Stephen King's gunslinger. Now, in the cold light of morning, he seemed older. Or tired.

He seemed Roland.

I sat up and he handed me a tin cup of coffee from off the fire. The handle was a little hot but the coffee was good.

"I'll head east today into Santa Ana," he said. "After that job, I should have enough to get the cattle and start a herd. If I can find them, I'll pasture them in the next few weeks on the hills south of Newport Beach, east of Irvine. There's a road, it's called

Jeffrey. Where the 405 intersects with Jeffrey, you'll see some low rolling hills. I'll be up in there. It shouldn't be too hard to find me up if you decide you want to go partners on the herd. That is, after you find who it is you're looking for, Jase. Or, if you don't find her."

I drank the coffee. We listened to the fire pop and crackle. The rain was beginning to slacken.

"How much does my share of the head bounty buy me in the herd?" I asked.

You can end the world of the investment banker, but you can't take the investment banker out of the end of the world.

He thought for a long moment.

"Fifty percent."

I suspected Chris of being generous.

"Alright then, we're partners. I've got to try and find my fiancée. If I do, or if I don't, I'll meet you up in the hills."

"Do you know where to look for her?"

"There's a hotel in Newport Beach near an outdoor mall. A place called Fashion Island. That was where she was, the last time I talked to her."

He reached down, picked up a folded map, and handed it to me.

"I marked up this map for you. Shows you where we've been and where you can meet me. I'm also giving you this."

He handed me a small olive-green object attached to the end of a braided loop of cord.

"It's a military compass. It'll tell you what direction you're headed. Do you know how to use a compass?"

I didn't.

"I'll show you before I leave. Keep it around your neck. I made the loop out of parachute cord I got off some National

Guardsmen for a bag of heads. It's soft so it won't rub your neck, but it also won't rip or break. Plus, like I said, I braided it, so it should hold up. Keep it around your neck when you travel. It's easier to keep checking your bearing that way. Also, compasses have a way of getting lost, ironically."

I held it in my hand. It was cold and compact. It felt comforting to have it. To have something that might tell me where I was, or where I might be going. Something that might lead me through the end of the world to Alex.

Chris rode away on Chief. I watched him disappear out the front gates of the stockade and into the gray mist of the soft drizzle that had settled over Beach Boulevard. He was a man on a horse riding through empty city streets in the rain.

"I hope that compass helps you find who you're looking for." That was the last thing he said to me. Now he was gone.

I felt alone again. Alone like I'd felt after all my friends, my fellow survivors, were gone and it was just me in the Tower. Alone all those weeks in the digging camps after… even though I was surrounded by others, who like me, had simply survived.

Now I'd become addicted to the company of others. Kyle and then Chris. If I could find Alex, I knew I would never leave her. Maybe we could raise cattle with Chris.

Those thoughts faded, and I felt the fear rise in me of walking out the back gate of the Stockade as I knew I must do in a few minutes.

Chris had shown me how to read the compass, how to get my bearings, how to shoot an azimuth. We'd used the map and plotted a course down into Newport Beach. Just five miles away.

"You ain't leaving with him?" asked Jackson the Stockade foreman.

I told him my plan.

"Ah, I wish you'da got here a day earlier. Reconstruction Team is operating out of there. Right on that site actually. Something big went down there on Day One of the outbreak and they're trying to find out what really happened and all."

I asked him if he had any idea what "really big" meant.

"No idea. The team leader said it was a top priority once the area had been cleared. Which really hasn't been a problem because of the Lady and her whole plan."

I asked him what he meant by that.

"Well, her crew came up outta that area. That's where the whole plan started. I was up in L.A. when they arrived, her and her crew. Said she had a plan to draw all the dead into a kill zone. They made a wide sweep down through Riverside, then up along the 55 right into Newport. Then they broke into teams, one took the coast road and the other the 405. Drew all of 'em up along the 710 and then right down the 101 into downtown. The rest is history."

"What happened to her?"

"After the battle... don't know," said the Stockade foreman. "I was busy getting a team together to come down here and set up this base. There was a rumor that a bunch of the dead were coming down outta the central valley, that's up north, above Los Angeles. So, the plan was for her and her crew to go up to the Grapevine and set up a new kill zone. Sounds like something she would've done from what I knew about her."

"She had a crew?"

"Yeah, but it was mainly her and some big African American dude. Bunch of other survivors they'd picked up also. Her own little army. How come you don't know this? Where've you been?"

"I was in New York."

"How'd you get out here?"

I told him. He wanted to know what New Orleans and Atlanta were like. Had they put together some kind of safe zone like Los Angeles?

I told him the truth.

He was quiet as he looked at the walls of the Stockade.

"Did you ever meet the Lady?" I asked.

"Honestly, I never met any of them, even her. Just heard the legend. All I know is she came from down here near the beach. Her and her crew were all driving off-road vehicles with guns and loudspeakers. They'd been driving around shooting up bands of infected and then retreating. That, and she looked like a rock star."

"Which one?" I didn't say anything. I didn't want to bias his account. If he said Pat Benatar or Carly Simon or even Shakira, then I could let it go.

"Blondie or someone. You know, that one that did She's Got the Look!"

That was Roxette.

He had it wrong.

But it was close enough.

Roxette, Blondie, Alex. Each could be taken for the other in a secondhand end of the world survivor account.

I was running for my rucksack. I felt my compass swinging across my chest, banging at my heart.

I could find her.

Maybe.

I wasn't afraid now. I wasn't afraid to walk out the back gate anymore. There was a chance I could find Alex. There was a chance she might still be alive. I would go to the hotel just five miles to the south. I had to eliminate that first, then I could go north and look for this Lady.

For Alex.

Beyond the back gate of the Stockade, I found myself walking along quiet streets that were once wide thoroughfares through busy commercial districts.

I headed west first, consulting my map, then moving forward.

Jackson had left me with a stern warning. Maybe I'd frightened him with what I told him of the east. His eyes had taken on a new look of fear and concern as he stared up at the walls of the Stockade, as if the walls weren't, or wouldn't ever be, high enough.

"Don't let your guard down out there. It still ain't completely safe," he called out as I headed through the back gate. "There're a few salvagers we ain't heard from in a week. So…"

So…

The morning mist and overcast was nice, and my fears from inside the Stockade had vanished. It felt good to be alone again in the thick silence of the drizzle and general isolation. To be moving again at a good pace, and on my own. Maybe headed toward Alex.

I turned left down a street that ran south and listened as the rain pattered quietly against the wet, empty street. Eventually its tempo picked up, and I waited in a darkened auto parts store where the windows had been smashed. I smelled a dead body, and as I looked through the aisles, I came upon a large lug wrench lying in a pool of dried blood. The back of the store was even darker and smelled of new tires and must.

I picked up the lug wrench.

I left, happy to be back out in the rain again.

Ahead, the road dipped into a ravine lined with towering eucalyptus trees. Their wet bark revealed beautiful whorls and stripes. The smell of the leaves was exotic and familiar all at once.

Later, at an intersection labeled Bristol and Adams, I saw the remains of two twisted cars scattered in pieces across the intersection. The bloated and swollen corpse of the driver lay pinned behind the wheel of a smashed Ferrari. The other vehicle, an SUV, high end, lay on its side. I covered my face with my arm and approached the Ferrari. The driver's face was ripped to pieces. What little remained of the top of his skull was like the caldera of a volcano. In his hand lay a pistol. I looked around and saw empty brass shell casings on the street and in the wreckage.

They had come for him. After the wreck. Pinned and still alive. He was driving fast to get somewhere quickly on that day everything went wrong for the world. Home maybe? Away, most likely. And then the accident. And then they'd come for him after the jarring crash, which had sent both vehicles spinning off in opposite, unplanned directions. As the sound of crunching metal and breaking plastic fades, as the chalk from the airbags blossoms in a dusty "smaff" across that last hot day of August three months ago, as the car alarms and horns begin their endless cries for rescue, the dead come. They come out of the gas station and the furniture store and the yogurt shop and the Chinese restaurant and the sports bar.

They come and Ferrari Man fires at them, even though his legs are crushed. He's not getting out of here alive and he knows it. He fires until there is just one bullet left.

And then he fires again.

I thought about taking the gun. I'd need to clean it. I'm sure there wasn't any ammo left, otherwise… the guy would have kept shooting.

I walked to the overturned black SUV. There was a pinned corpse stuck halfway under the vehicle.

Someone didn't have a gun to fight the dead off.

There's no head.

Someone else has already claimed their fifty CalDollars.

I wondered how long the SUV driver had lain there, perpetually tormented, unendingly pinned.

I checked my map. Down the street, I could see the small freeway that passed by the airport and led right down into Newport Beach.

I went back to the crumpled Ferrari and took the gun. It was the kind that didn't have a cylinder where the bullets waited. It didn't have a hammer either. It was matte black.

Walking away from the wreck, I wondered how long they would lay there. In the rain. In the spring to come. In the summer that followed. Someday, someone would come and sweep up the wreck down to the broken glass, and no one would know what had happened there on that long-lost day when everything went so wrong.

And was there someone waiting for each of those intersected lives? Waiting in a refugee camp, or behind stockade walls, or buried in the red dirt underneath City Center?

Waiting to be found whether probably dead or almost impossibly alive.

They would never know what had happened at the intersection.

I walked faster as I walked away from that place.

The sky began to clear into blue patches, as white clouds moved briskly in the autumn breeze.

I climbed the freeway off-ramp and found a wide, clean, spacious curving road that wound its way up onto the coast.

I could see the small range of hills off to the south that Chris had shown me on the map.

I could live in those green hills on rainy days like today.

I thought about steak.

Another mile along the highway, and I saw large white tents set up across the road. The road descended into a large cut in the earth and the tents, several of them, lay flapping in the grass of a wide median.

I saw the bodies when I got close. They rested inside black plastic body bags in stacks five high. The road was littered with the remains of burnt out flares.

I pulled back the flap on the largest tent. Inside, I found what was to be expected. Dull metal tables and trays. IV stands. Bodies not in bags.

I closed the flap and circled around the shuddering tents that stuttered and snapped in the afternoon breeze. White clouds raced inland, filled with the smell of the ocean. The patches of blue sky above seemed clean, and the antithesis of the body bags and what must be in them.

I followed the highway beyond the tents and soon came to the off-ramp that would lead me to Jamboree Boulevard and then to the hotel. I checked the map. I estimated another two miles. I drank some of the bottled water I'd taken from the Stockade and adjusted my ruck sack. I wanted to be somewhere before nightfall. Before it rained again. The hotel seemed like it might be the place.

That is, as I'm writing this, if the hotel I'm looking at, the one with the sign reading The Pacific, looked anything like a hotel anymore.

I'm writing this from the campfire at the Reconstruction basecamp. It's just past dusk. Out to sea, it is still daylight in a milky, almost forlorn way. The wind is racing in off the coast. A cold front is moving in from Alaska. Cold wind and rain are ahead for the next few days.

The "hotel" looms above us. It's a blackened spire with chunks of concrete torn out of every available space of wall. Almost like polka-dots. The entire place looks like a warzone, more than any-place I've ever seen, even New York. It looks like artillery hit this place. It looks like every machinegun in the world was fired at random in every direction. There is not one place where there is not churned, bullet-ridden earth, pockmarked walls, sprays of concrete, shattered glass, chunks of broken rocks, and half-demolished buildings. Not one place. And there are bodies. Lots of bodies.

A sea of bodies.

When I entered the mall complex earlier, I could see the crews placing yellow markers near the bodies. There are tents at the base camp.

The workers stopped as I approached.

I met Karen. She is a short, stocky, red-haired woman.

She's the leader of the Reconstruction Team.

She listened to my story.

She said they would try to help me find Alex if they could.

I tried not to look at all the bodies in the parking lot between the mall and the hotel.

~~November 31st~~ December 1st

I never thought about the fact that there aren't 31 days in November. I know you just looked at your cell phone or the calendar, or whatever there is left to remind us of the numbering of our days. Now, I am forced to write my own dates, like some savage.

Just kidding. It occurs to me that my dates might be all wrong. I know there's an October 31st. But is there a September 31st?

Karen, the crew leader for the Reconstruction team, won't let me enter the hotel.

She's probably right. In the light of day, the hotel looks like a block of Swiss cheese. It looks like something you would see in TIME. Something out of a battlefield reporter's notebook. There are corpses everywhere. You can't tell whether they were infected or not. Every one of them has been out here for over three months.

Three months as of yesterday.

The talk, my Reconstruction buddy Ramos tells me, is that this is where the outbreak inside the U.S. initially went down.

If that's the case, then what are my chances of finding Alex? Could she have survived ground zero?

Is she the Lady?

Staring at all these dead bodies reminds me that a living Alex is almost too much to hope for.

I'm getting my hopes down.

Up would be good right about now.

I'm convinced they're going to find her out in that body-swollen parking lot between the mall and the hotel.

But when I think about that possibility, might that not be better than some of the other outcomes I've witnessed?

Ragged and mangled, chasing a train through a dirty and tangled forest.

Swinging from a light post, the plaything of Low Men.

Alone and crawling across a child's playground in the middle of the night.

We go out in pairs, Ramos and me, all the others like us. We find the marker we've been assigned to. We lay the body out. I do the writing. I enter the data on the form, writing on a clipboard. Ramos tells me what to write.

Position of Body?

"Supine. Means on her stomach, man," he says in his vato-homeboy Mexican accent.

Obvious wounds?

"Soccer ball-sized wound to the stomach, oh, and a bullet wound to the head, man."

Obvious signs of infection?

"Umm, hard to tell, man. No wait, she's got black crud under her fingernails."

So what do I write?

"Write that, Homes! Black crud under fingernails."

Okay. Personal effects?

"She's got a bracelet. Let's see, and a ring. Earrings too."

Identification?

"Nothing in her pockets. You rarely find anything on the women. Cause they usually had like purses. It's a sure sign they're infected if they don't have a purse on 'em, Homes."

Then we bag her.

We have gloves and face masks. But you can feel everything through the thin medical gloves. And the mask doesn't block out the smell.

She was once a living, breathing girl, I think, as we place her in the bag.

We carry her back and check her in. She's un-bagged, photographed, re-bagged, and then we stack her with the rest of... the dead, that are waiting to be burned in an open pit currently being dug in a vacant lot down by the coast road.

We get another marker number and we go find…

- Unknown Female.
- David Chang.
- Unknown Female.
- Unknown Female.
- Unknown Male.
- Tom Watson.

And…

At the end of the day, I asked Karen how long it might be until I can get into the hotel and look for Alex, or find clues that lead to where she might have gone.

Karen said she was making a priority out of my request, and as soon as the structure engineer cleared the Reconstruction crews to enter the lobby, they would try to get the hotel computer up and running.

She asked that I be patient.

It's night now. Ramos and I share a tent with another team. There are showers set up and a field kitchen. I didn't think I'd be hungry this evening, but I was. We had spaghetti and garlic bread. Still no fresh produce.

I am dying for a salad.

December 2nd

- Kevin White.
- Unknown Male.
- Unknown Male.
- Unknown Female.
- Unknown Male.

- Unknown Female.
- Ramon Gutierrez.

We had showers. We had mystery meat cheeseburgers and fries. We also got two beers each.

December 3rd

After working all day, the rain came up off the sea and battered the Reconstruction site. We've almost cleared the entire parking lot. Tomorrow we'll be moving into the mall.

When I got back to base camp, Karen walked me over to the hotel. It must have been really nice, once. Giant palm-filled urns, teak furniture, open and airy on sunny, Southern California days. Now it was dark. Fallen leaves had been swept in from the outside by the wind and the rain. The once luxurious lobby furniture was torn to pieces.

"Be careful," Karen said as we stepped over gritty, shattered glass. "There are splinters everywhere."

We went behind the front desk. A dim blue light came from a working computer. I looked at the screen briefly, hoping it would be Alex's check-in info.

"We're trying to get the server to reboot, but the partition is corrupted. It's gonna take time," explained Karen. "We're hoping we can get into the backup and find a guest list. Maybe. Ronny thinks it'll be up around midnight. That's the best I can do for you, Jason. I'm sorry it's not more."

I stared at the slowly advancing bar on the screen.

"Thank you," I mumbled to her, watching that bar as though the answer to the meaning of life lay at its completion. "I'll wait. If that's okay?"

She said it was.

Eventually, Ronny appeared. He'd been down in the room where the hotel kept the server. We sat and had some warm sodas from the hotel bar. We each had one and talked about computers. Or rather, I listened about computers.

Karen brought us two trays of ChiliMac and we ate. They talked Reconstruction business. The business of putting it all back together again. It seemed overwhelming by the amount of paperwork they were discussing. I didn't need to ask what the point of it all was. Of Reconstruction. I was the point. As much as was possible, they were to answer one question. Could they find out "who" was "where" on the day everything changed? And more importantly, what had happened to that "who"? It would be recorded on a sheet of paper by people like Ramos and me. It would go into a database. Eventually people would be able to type in the name of the "who" they'd lost. The "who" they'd been searching for.

And maybe, someone who had not been found, would be.

Finally.

Then the searcher might know, and if not, there was the massive photographic database to search. But that seemed impossible.

At fifteen to one in the morning, Ronny cracked the partition and we got the master guest list. Alex came up as soon as we typed in her name.

Room 709.

Karen looked at me. The look said, "I don't believe it. I didn't actually believe you, until now."

And then there was a look that said something like, "Why you? Why do you get to know?"

But maybe she was just worried I'd want to do exactly what I wanted to do at that moment.

"Uh-Uh, Jason. No. The engineer has to clear each floor before we can go up. This building is hanging by a thin thread. Give us some time, Jason. Can you do that?" Her voice came from far away. "Can you give us time?"

I looked at her and did not see her.

"I'll put you and Ramos on the building crew if you promise you'll wait. Promise me you won't crack room 709 unless I'm there. Promise me, Jason."

I promised.

December 4th

Building Crew all day.

We spent the day clearing the lobby. There were bodies hidden in the strangest places. Under tables. Behind the once opulent bar. In the pantry. One crew found a "mover" locked in a meat locker. It was frozen, but still there, if you know what I mean. I think it had been a cook.

We had ChiliMac again.

December 5th

We did the first five floors today. We found one body. It was an easy day. It felt warm outside, and most of the day we just stood around in the stairwell, waiting to be cleared to work on the next floor. Most of the rooms are still in pristine condition, as if they'd been ready for check-in when it all went down. Then there is the shattered glass and large-caliber bullet holes in the pristine bedspreads and along painted and decorated walls.

Ramos told me his story today.

So, maybe in California, things are different. I guess people are more open here. They don't seem to mind sharing how the world ended for them.

He was in a prison he simply called "Tehachapi" when it all went sideways. The prison was relatively safe. They offered parole to everyone who was willing to help the Army down in Los Angeles. Ramos took the offer. There weren't too many other takers. Most of the prisoners knew what was going on outside and felt safer behind the walls and the razor wire.

Anyway, the bus they were being transported down to Los Angeles in stopped for gas at a place called Lancaster out in the high desert. The guard and the driver got off and were met by a dark Mercedes. Each received a briefcase from some La Familia-types and disappeared. Then some homeboys came onto the bus and said they were releasing everyone. They were just after one specific guy who'd volunteered along with the rest back in Tehachapi. They took him off first while Ramos and the others watched through the dirty, shuttered window slats of the prison bus. They shot the guy in the parking lot. After that, they released the rest and drove off. Ramos said at that point everyone just scattered. He and two others formed up, all of them close to a real parole, and decided to continue on as planned and join the Army.

They made it as far as the San Fernando Valley when one of them got bit. They took him into a pharmacy just as things were really deteriorating. The owner of the pharmacy locked the doors and made everyone stay inside. Except the guy who got bit. For the next three weeks they lived inside the pharmacy. One day this girl, Yessina, opened a side door on her guard shift and snuck out to find her family. She didn't lock the door, and an hour later, three Infected had wandered in and gotten to a couple of the people. Yessina returned crying about what she'd seen at her family's house. She said the streets were mostly quiet.

Now they had a couple of sick people who were getting sicker by the minute, and Yessina had an injury to her arm that looked suspiciously like a bite. She said she'd gotten hurt jumping over the back fence of her family's house.

The manager kicked all of them out including Yessina.

A week later, the infected were hammering at every entrance to the pharmacy, which had steel roll-down doors. Ramos got onto the roof and could see the infected everywhere. They were swarming toward the pharmacy. It was evident that the sheer weight of them would soon crumple the thin, roll-down doors inward. Seams were already starting to appear in the sheet metal.

The noise didn't stop.

That was when the manager took a bunch of pills and committed suicide. A few hours later, he started walking around again and tried to kill the other survivors. Over the next three days, one by one, the others followed the manager's lead. Except someone had found a gun and it kept making the rounds. In the end, it was just Ramos. He kept going to the roof to look for help. He started to build barricades throughout the store so he could surrender as little space as possible. He built concentric rings of shelving all the way to the stairwell that let out onto the roof. The only weapons he had were some box cutters, useless against those things, he said, a kids' baseball bat from the toy section, and some Molotov cocktails he made from what was left of the liquor aisle. He knew it was a death sentence to use the Molotovs inside the store.

One day, he went to the roof after he heard some explosions coming from across the valley. He couldn't tell exactly where the explosions were coming from, but it looked to be near downtown Los Angeles, which he couldn't see because of the hills in the way. Then he saw plumes of smoke and fighter jets racing away.

"I said to myself, good for them," he told me as we sat in the stairwell of The Pacific Hotel drinking warm sodas and waiting to be used on the next floor.

"I was really happy for them over in downtown. It felt good to know somebody was finally fighting back. I'd just watched a whole bunch of people off themselves because they were hopeless, so it felt pretty good to see those explosions."

Then he told me about the Lady.

"A day later, the Lady showed up with her crew. Homes, I thought I was saved."

Ramos heard the machinegun fire from inside the pharmacy while he was eating a bag of barbecued sunflower seeds. He ran up to the roof in time to see three vehicles, two Hummers and a monster truck blaring rock music, firing guns and throwing grenades at the infected. By the time Ramos reached the roof, the Hummers and monster truck were pulling back down the street. The infected were staggering away from the building, stumbling after the trucks.

Ramos checked the sides of the pharmacy, lowered himself down to a dumpster, and ran for it. Twenty-four hours later, he made it to the still-burning plumes of black smoke piling up over downtown. He found the Army and the burn piles.

As we waited in the stairwell, listening to the end of Ramos's story, we could hear someone above us demolishing a wall with a sledgehammer.

Then there was a single gunshot.

"Must have found a live one," said Ramos.

We listened and waited for the radio to pop and the chatter of a status report.

I asked, "Didn't you ever feel like giving up?" I was thinking about the "live one" they'd found. I was thinking about Alex.

"Nah, no way man," he said quickly in his Latino vato home-boy accent. "I was free. I wasn't gonna give that up, Homes. Not ever again."

When we got back to base camp that night, there were fresh strawberries. One of the cooks had been out foraging and found them growing wild.

I have never tasted anything better in my life. Sorry churros.

December 6th

Karen pulled me off building crew just as we were checking in this morning.

"Engineer cleared floor seven last night. I guess we'd better go take a look at room 709."

I looked at Ramos as if I had something to say. But I had no idea at that moment what I'd wanted to say. I think I just needed a friend. A human face to check in with before everything changed.

"You can do it," he said.

I was grateful for that.

My legs felt weak as we climbed the stairs. I wanted to throw up. I felt dizzy. I felt like I was on a rollercoaster that I didn't want to be on. We approached the door to Room 709 and I could see it was open. I heard Karen's footsteps on the carpet come to a halt behind me.

I pushed back the splintered remains of the door.

No Alex.

Bottles. Lots of them.

I found her bag.

I felt my compass dangling from my neck as I searched her luggage for anything. I tucked the compass inside my shirt.

Her clothing.

Things I had bought her. Things I knew.

I found another bag. Black canvas duffel.

Men's clothing.

Men's deodorant.

Men's razors and aftershave.

Hair care products for the African American Male.

I don't know what to make of that.

December 7th

The shock is still setting in. I don't know whether to grieve and tell myself she's dead...

Or keep looking for her.

Even if she is the Lady... who was she with?

And when I think about all that someone else and their hair care products can imply, I remember... I'm the hypocrite.

I didn't work today.

I borrowed a bike and rode down MacArthur Boulevard. I was the only one on that lonely road. I exited at a wide curve and took University. For a while, the road ran alongside an estuary next to the University of California at Irvine.

The silence gave me a case of the willies, and I wondered how many of the infected were in and amongst the mud and reeds.

In the swamps.

Waiting.

Stuck. Trapped somehow.

I heard the lone cry of a bird, and later I saw a heron standing motionless in the water.

Would they go after herons?

When I got close to the place Chris had marked on the map, I found myself beneath gently rolling hills that fled away to the south.

It was cold and the wind moved the grass in great waves.

There were no cows.

No Chris either.

December 8th

I'm back with the Reconstruction Team.

I work for the photographer now. When the crews bring in each corpse and lay it out, we photograph it. Mainly Ramos and I just unzip the bag, wait while its photographed, zip the bag back up and carry the corpses between piles. Ramos is glad we're off building detail. The photographer is quiet. He doesn't say much.

The bodies.

There are lots of them. If you allow yourself, you can tell exactly what they were thinking in that last moment before...

They are peaceful, they are shocked, and sometimes they are angry.

Most of them have head wounds. Which unofficially indicates they were infected.

If Alex is here, then I'll find her. At night I plan to go through the database of photographs from this site. If she's here, I will find her.

December 9th

Going through the photographic database didn't take long. She hasn't been photographed yet. There's only one more section of bodies to bring out from the mall. Then I guess there'll be some clean-up work and we'll be reassigned. "We"? Did I just join the Army again?

I asked a few people if they knew the Lady. Most of the survivors don't, but a few of them fought at the battle of City Center. Same description. They also say she had a crew. A big black guy in particular.

December 10th

I snuck back into the hotel last night.

Long after lights out.

It was foggy.

Even warm.

I waited until they'd shut off the generators for the night. The big sodium lights that ring the perimeter went dark, and before the guards could get their night vision goggles adjusted, I ran across the wide street and into the dense garden surrounding the hotel.

It was dark and shadowy in the lobby. I found the stairwell and climbed to the seventh floor. Once inside the stairwell, I used my flashlight. There was dark blood on the walls. Chunks of concrete. The stairs groaned in places as I climbed higher.

On the seventh floor, I found Alex's room again. The room faces away from the camp so I used my flashlight to search, knowing the guards couldn't see the light. I sat down on the carpet and looked at the room.

I needed to know. I needed to make up my mind about whether I was going to go on believing that somewhere out there Alex might still be alive, or resign myself to the knowledge that she was dead, and do what comes next.

Which was either start a new life, or…

I went through the black canvas duffel bag.

The guy's bag.

There were hair care products for African Americans. There weren't any condoms.

I went through her things. I found her calendar. Wedding plans. Circles around important dates. On the day we were supposed to get married she'd written, "Yayyy!"

I put one of her blouses up to my nose and inhaled.

I couldn't smell anything.

I've smelled too much death.

The bed was made. I mean it wasn't perfect, but no one had slept in it.

I found a half-full bottle of cognac amongst all the empties. It was under the bed.

Why was there so much liquor?

That was Alex.

She liked to party.

I mean, she could cross the line. But it wasn't like she had a problem. Still, this was a lot of liquor.

I wondered if maybe someone other than Alex had been here in this room, holding out.

Maybe Alex had been somewhere else when it all went down.

Whoever held up here, like we did in the Tower, this was their liquor, their black duffel bag, their African American styling gel.

Is that a story I can live with?

If she was having an affair, where was her ring? I spent two week's commissions on that ring.

Most people's yearly salary.

I went through her things and found a small compartment where she kept her passport and another piece of jewelry. A locket with a picture of a woman I didn't recognize. Alex's grandmother maybe? I knew the locket had been important to her.

Can I believe this? Can I believe that if Alex were in the room with another man she would have put her ring in this pouch where she kept mementos from her grandmother? Can I believe that it's not here and therefore it's on her finger, wherever that finger is?

I looked for her smartphone. I went to the bathroom, crossing the stiff and stale carpet on my hands and knees. I went through every hollow-sounding drawer that opened. I knew I should smell pine and wood and maybe even cedar and dust, but still, the stench of death wouldn't let me. I searched behind the bullet-shattered TV. Behind the one remaining designer lamp. Out on the balcony. No phone.

Bullet holes had stitched themselves across the walls inside the room.

Why the shooting?

In the Tower, a busy Manhattan office tower, it felt as though we'd been abandoned. Here, someone had made an effort to kill whoever was inside this room. Granted, the shooting, when you looked at the whole mall complex, seemed indiscriminate and excessive. But why smaller bullet holes in this room? Alex's room.

In the Tower, we'd just kept going up.

I looked upward.

Whoever survived, if Alex had survived, they would have gone up. Like we did. I might find her up there. I might find a dead cell phone there. I might find her ring there on another survivor. If she'd been killed, maybe it was something a survivor might have taken. I could check their pockets. If I find the ring, or the phone, I'll know she made it that far.

My heart was thumping heavily as I climbed the steps in the stairwell. The top floor was still red-tagged.

It hadn't been cleared yet.

I slipped in under the tape that should have warned me off.

The door to the suite had once been barricaded—badly—by my standards. On the other side, splintered hotel furniture lay in ruins. It was a suite. There were bullet holes everywhere. There were two bodies. One was a para-military type in blue combat fatigues with large dark stains on his chest, hanging from a rope dangling off the roof. The other was Matt. Alex's boss.

He was bloated and naked.

I'd seen enough infected to know he'd been one. One, that is, before the bullet hole in his head.

I searched the whole floor. No phone, no ring.

This morning, just after dawn, I slipped back into the camp. A sentry stopped me. I told him I'd gone over to grab a flashlight I'd left in the hotel the day before.

I reported for sick call and slept until noon. I grabbed lunch and sat on my bunk for the rest of the afternoon.

Thinking.

December 11th

Even if she was cheating on me, I still need to find her.

To be honest, I've mixed up cheating with death these past few days.

Maybe it was easier that way.

I'd liked the idea of Alex waiting for me to find her, to rescue her. Then I'm shattered by the fact someone else might have rescued her. Or maybe she even rescued herself.

The fine print on my own personal "Dark Tower" quest was beginning to mess me up. But now I have a little clarity and I think I've come to a realization. The truth is… I don't care if she was with someone before or after everything started. There are justifications for me accepting both scenarios. The only thing that matters is that I find her. If she's the one the kid on the steps told me about, the Lady, then I can find her. And if I can find her, then… maybe we can build something again. Something new.

All the corpses have been cleared and we're pulling out for three days' leave in L.A. Then we get our new assignment. Karen came and talked to me. She knew I'd been in the building. She said she understood. She would have gone in too to find news of someone she loved. She also said I was never officially part of her crew, so it wasn't going in any of the paperwork. If I want to join, she could find a place for me on the next assignment.

I told her I'd let her know.

She gave me a check drawn on the Bank of New California for my services with the Reconstruction Crew.

Tonight I went out beyond the perimeter into the mall parking lot. It's so quiet I can hear the surf pounding the coast down by the ocean. The sound is distant and yet intense, like a clock in the hall.

I stood looking at the cratered parking lot. The Swiss-cheese hotel. The remains of the mall.

If Alex was here, I didn't find her.

I didn't feel, in my heart, that she was there anymore.

For whatever that's worth.

December 16th

The wind feels good.

Every so often, up here in the Central Valley, you smell rain. Beyond that, sometimes you smell death. We've passed a lot of towns. From the highway, up in our convoy of buses, you see the barricades that didn't hold, the burnt cars, sometimes even corpses still sprawled across the county roads and fields. We pass small towns where corpses lie blackened and charred in the middle of intersections. Our Reconstruction team is being sent to a gas station town called Turleyville to reconstruct a reported survivor holdout. The others call it a Last Stand. Officially, in Reconstruction paperwork, it is known as a Siege Event.

We survivors all have our passports stamped with that one.

I have yet to meet one person, living, that was not part of a Siege Event. A Last Stand. The world is now populated by Last Standers. We all have that in common.

Apparently the people in Turleyville didn't make it. So we're being sent there to find the IDs, bury the dead, and tell their story. That's how Karen summarized the mission.

It's rained most of the journey. Small, soft, wet spring rain, though spring should be some time away still.

We want it to be spring.

We want to start again.

But in reality, it's just the beginning of winter.

After we got back to L.A. from Newport Beach, we were turned loose on the "Zona" as it's being called. The "Zona" is the barricaded area in the southern part of downtown Los Angeles. The Market District.

Karen caught me just as everyone fled the yard where we'd parked the buses and trucks.

"This little rest will be good for you. But come back. That'll be good for you too."

I said I'd think about it.

I found a small hotel and checked in for the night. I slept sideways on the bed, my feet hanging off, because I was so tired. I'd lain down for just a moment after a hot shower, and when I awoke it was late evening. Somewhere down the hall I heard someone laughing. Or crying. For most people, there is little to laugh about.

I went out into the night and the brightly-lit streets. There was a big party going on.

I got drunk at a taco stand and sat talking with the owner and his daughter. We talked about the Yankees. We drank. I ate tacos all night. His daughter—pretty, young, slim, Latina, worked the grill—and occasionally when a group of revelers would stop for food he would jump behind the cart and help her.

But mostly we talked about the Yankees. He was a Dodgers fan, even back when they had been in Brooklyn, so he knew about the Yankees as every Dodgers fan must, or so he told me.

We didn't talk about what had happened to us.

We didn't tell our stories.

We talked about the Yankees.

We talked about Reggie Jackson and Thurman Munson and Billy Martin.

I didn't want to talk about Derek Jeter because I knew I would think of the Derek Jeter Monday Morning Meeting Bat.

Then I would think of the Tower.

At dawn, it was time to close.

Mostly drunk, I helped them clean up. With a hose, I sprayed down the walkway where they kept their cart, washing away all the spilled carne asada and tortillas and cheese the other drunken revelers had left in the wake of their carousing. Then we walked back a few streets to a small garage and I helped them load their cooking tools into it.

"We have a place in Hilltop. Come and have a proper breakfast with us," offered the old man.

I tried to decline, but even the daughter clutched at my arm and dragged me along with them. I felt the extra squeeze she gave that her father did not see.

We had chilaquiles.

I've never had chilaquiles before.

After breakfast, the old man poured a few fingers of tequila into cut crystal glasses for the three of us, then retired to the enclosed porch where he said he would sleep most of the day.

I sat watching the remains of the gigantic meal being cleared by his daughter.

When it was done, she nodded from the kitchen, a dishtowel over one shoulder, and led me to the back of the house.

We lay down fully clothed. Before I could even begin to kiss her lips, we'd drifted into sleep, comforted by the tight warmth we felt as we held onto each other's bodies for more than just passion.

For security.

For comfort.

For the touch that said life.

When I woke, she was gone. I lay in her room. There were posters of musicians and cars. There were pictures of her and a young man and a baby.

I got up and walked to the rear door of the house and went out into the backyard. The afternoon was thick with heat and buzzing insects. I climbed over the fence and found an old trash-littered alley. I left there and never looked back.

I wasn't ready.

And my guess is she wasn't either.

It'll be a long time before anybody is ready again.

I drank and slept in my hotel room. A day and the next one passed. I wandered the streets looking at the faces of the living, knowing that each face had seen its fair share of death.

I stood in front of a chain link fence, studying the faces of the missing in the collage that had grown there.

In truth, I was ready to head south again. I would find Chris and start a new life. A downpour had begun to fall on that last afternoon in L.A., and with its coming, the ongoing festival had seemingly disappeared into the rain-swollen gutters.

In the early evening, I found an old warehouse that served beer at a bar which kept watch over old and battered pool tables. Rain dripped into strategically placed pans and buckets.

I was down to my last ten CalDollars.

Did I ever mention I had seven-point-five-million offshore? It's not important now. It just seemed funny to me as I stood there figuring how many beers I could get for ten CalDollars.

It was later, when the thunder started to roll across the city and the rain came down in sheets that a few drunks, nice guys actually, began to talk about the Lady.

What they said changed everything for me.

What they said gave me hope.

Alex is the Lady.

I believe it now that I have written it down.

I didn't believe it before. I'd wanted to. But I didn't. I listened to all their stories about the Lady. A lot about the battle at City Center. The drunks told me a patchwork collection of short stories, episodes and limited-edition graphic novels regarding a hot chick with a rock star haircut who had risen, led a crew of fighters, fought back, and survived the end of the world.

Alex was a leader.

Alex was a fighter.

She looked like a rock star from the eighties.

Alex could have had a crew.

One of them could have been the black guy who used hair care products for the African American male.

They'd first appeared down in Orange County, rescuing bands of survivors from off rooftops and behind crumbling barricades.

Her plan had led to the battle at City Center.

Most of the stories were secondhand accounts. Guys who had been on the fringe or knew some other guy that had been there when she did that thing, or the other thing, that saved the day. One kid had fought right alongside her at City Center.

"I told myself I'd run when she did," said the kid.

But she never did.

"Someone's screaming bloody murder down in the machine-gun pits. There's a gunshot. Above all that moaning and growling the dead are making, I can hear some sorry chungo screaming plain as day that he's bit."

The kid paused as he drank from the beer I'd bought him.

"Then someone says we gotta pull back, there's too many of 'em. And I'm thinkin' to myself, hell yeah, now there's a sensible man. But she just says, 'Then leave your weapons and get the hell out of here. I'm not running today. This is it. Right here, right now!' So, I stuck. And for about twenty minutes, I thought we were done for. We were dumping everything into that avalanche of dead people and they just kept on comin'. I saw a jet come in way too low and strafe 'em. Then the pilot got creamed all over the side of City Hall and half of Old Town."

"But we stopped 'em. We stopped 'em right there at the top of the steps."

The kid took a long pull off his beer, finishing it.

"Lady just wouldn't run."

"Where'd she go after that?" I asked. I hadn't said anything until now. "I mean, what happened after the battle?"

"She led the Army, the new Army that is, up into the Central Valley. Last I heard, they were advancing on San Francisco. They clear that out and that'll be something. I never met one survivor that's come from anywhere north of Bakersfield. I heard its bad up in the northern part of the state. Real bad, in fact."

Everyone in the bar agreed.

It was bad up there.

I admit, even now, lying in my cot here at our new Reconstruction camp near the AmeriCal Gas Station in Central California, there could be every chance in the world it's not Alex. But, if there is even the slightest chance in the world it is her, then I've got to try and find her. If Alex is the Lady, I've got to find her. I'll tell her everything. And if she'll let me… I'll live with her for the rest of my life.

We start the Reconstruction of Turleyville tomorrow.

December 17th

What remains?

What happened at the AmeriCal Gas Station and Mart in Turleyville could be a…

It could be the story of what happened to all of us.

The rotting dead are piled high against the doors of the little convenience market. The windows are boarded up and look rust-stained, though we all know it is not rust that has left these stains on the Big Box Store plywood that someone might have used for a tree house or a room addition if everything that happened, had not happened. Stray corpses wait out near the pumps. Across the road. In the middle of the streets.

We begin to collect these. Them. We are working systematically. My first corpse is a woman. A girl. Tina Martinez. She doesn't look Hispanic. Her teeth are black. Bared. Her eyes vacant. There are dark circles where the fever consumed her beauty and then withered what remained. She wears stained jeans and a shirt that must have once been white. There is a high-powered rifle wound, so Ramos tells me he would like to bet, that has taken off the side of her scalp. What's left of her brain lies along the dry grass median that separates the pumps from the road.

The Reconstruction team is smaller this time. Only ten two-person teams. Karen, and Guy her right hand man, oversee our work. We work the street corpses for the morning. The corpses that didn't make it to the barricaded door of the station.

After lunch we head for the gas station. The dead lay piled inward against the splintered remains of the main door. As though they had all fallen through suddenly. Beneath these are more of them.

In all, there are almost a hundred. I never would've guessed that many.

We lay them out in rows and settle to filling out our forms, then bagging the personal effects. By late afternoon, we have them stacked in body bags at the rear of the gas station.

Karen enters the darkened hole that leads into the barricaded gas station alone, and calls out to see if anyone's in there. She's holding a pistol and flashlight, even though a bright orange tag indicates the Army has cleared this location. The tag flutters in the afternoon breeze.

We return to our tent camp in the open field nearby, where spring planting will not be done this year, and already the Ops Tent is lit by the blue glow of computers uploading our forms. The workers inside stare into screens with that same pasty dead look that the bodies, in many cases, out back wear.

We get cold showers and a hot meal. But no one feels like eating. Some people play cards.

I think I'll turn in.

I couldn't sleep, so I took a walk and ended up in the Ops Tent. I looked at the big map. There are markers around the Bay Area. All around San Francisco to our northwest.

I asked what they mean, the markers.

Some markers, blue triangles, represent The Army of the New California Republic. Other markers and marks, red ragged lines, red skulls and crossbones, giant red circles, represent the dead in all their various types of groupings.

There is a lot of red.

Far more than there is blue.

Karen tells me Army radio traffic has been quiet for a week. She says she's nervous about that. Those blue markers are the last known positions of the Army. The distance between us, the gas station town of Turleyville, and those blue triangles surrounding the southern edge of the San Francisco Bay Area, is not very far. They are all that stand between us and a sea of red.

I understand Karen's nervousness.

I wonder which of those blue triangles represents Alex.

I tried to press Karen for more. But I could see it had been a bad idea in the first place to tell me what she'd already told me. That much is obvious.

December 18th

Ramos, myself, and one other team went into the gas station this morning with Karen.

Our initial assignment was to find out what happened in each section of the "Last Stand".

"Siege Event Details" it states on a form at the top of Karen's clipboard.

Who survived and how long?

Who turned and when?

Who are… I mean were, the survivors, as opposed to the infected?

There is a section to annotate any personal notes that were left behind by the survivors. These are to be recorded and acted upon in the event other survivors fled to another location. Maybe they're there now, waiting to be rescued.

No one believed Karen when she explained that to us. She told us there are probably groups out there who don't know the

tide has turned. That government services are coming back on-
line. They're still out there surviving. How many years will we
go on finding groups like that who've lived, thinking like left behind Japanese soldiers on the Islands of the Pacific during and
after World War Two, that their world has ended, that the war
continues?

There were more corpses inside the store.

Most of them were infected. We checked for long-term exposure to the virus and all met the criteria.

There was one guy, a redneck type, behind the counter, holding a double-barreled shotgun. His head was missing.

At the back of the store, we found the entrance to the beer
cooler. In the beer cooler, we found empty rifles and empty pis-
tols. We also found the partial corpses of the survivors.

The teams came in and removed the corpses to the parking
lot for identification and forms. As they did, we worked through
the story with Karen.

"Survivors?" she asked.

"None," she answered.

"Suicides? Ramos?"

"I don't know, Karen," he said, his Vato accent thick, his voice
quiet like he didn't want to be there. As if he didn't want to be
involved. But then, "It looks like the hillbilly offed himself early
on. Maybe he got bit. Then the three in the cooler must have kept
fighting until they ran outta bullets. I'd count them as suicides."

"Why?"

"They had the guns and the ammo. That beer cooler door
would've held forever. But those things would have come through
that shattered display glass. Looks like they did too. If it helps
with how long they lasted, there wasn't much beer left."

"Okay good. I'll buy," said Karen, as she made notes on

her clipboard. "But not the hillbilly. If he killed himself, they would've wrapped the body up and stuck him on the roof or somewhere else. But the three in the cooler sounds like a likely story. You guys have anything else to add?"

I did.

"I found some tick marks on the counter where the hot dogs were sold. Four sets of five and two individual marks. So twenty-two. Might mean they held out for twenty two days."

Karen looked at me for a long moment.

"Twenty-two days." She nodded as she wrote on her form. "That could be a record."

"How's that?" asked Ramos.

"How long they survived. Twenty-two days seems like the longest one we've found so far."

Ramos scratched his head.

"But they failed. We hold the record, Karen. Each of us here survived longer than that. We're the winners because we're still alive."

We're the winners.

December 20th

It's well after midnight. Midnight of the twentieth. But I'm writing this for yesterday. It's my last entry. I'll leave this for the record. The record of who I was.

I'm going now.

Late on the night of the 18th, Guy comes into the tent.

"Get up everyone, hurry. We've got infected coming in from every direction!"

For a moment I think he means they're outside, in the fields and crossing the interstate, shambling across the low-lying fog through the tall dead grass.

But that's not the case.

The Army needs help.

They've been pushed back to a town called Manteca, which is north of here. When we're all outside, Karen tells us a huge "train" of infected are bearing down out of the San Francisco Bay Area. A last-ditch defense is being set up in Manteca. They load us into the buses and we're off into the night.

When we get to the defense, they hand us shovels and tell us to get to work building dirt walls along the off ramps leading back along the freeway, away from an overpass.

Earthmovers are shoveling mountains of dirt along the off and on ramps of the overpass and into the gap beneath. The plan is to make a small castle using the high overpass as a sort of castle gate. The sides, rear, and directly underneath the overpass will become walls of scrapped dirt towering over pits from which the earth had been taken.

They plan to "hold the line" here.

We worked for the rest of that night, shoveling under bright gas-powered construction lights on long poles. Near dawn, we got coffee and cereal bars.

I couldn't help thinking it was my last meal.

The rest of the Army started coming into "the castle" in ragged bands. A small opening beneath the overpass was left exposed while a bulldozer waited by a mound of dirt to close up the gap at a moment's notice.

The Army had wounded. There had been an accidental explosion at a bridge over in the hills that lead to the bay. Men and women had been crushed by debris, both flying and falling. Their plan, the Army, had been to set up a defense at the Altamont pass. But the accidental explosion had derailed that plan, and now a huge swarm of undead were trailing the Army as it retreated out of the bay and straight into our "Castle". If the corpses broke through the Central Valley, all the cleared areas, even Los Angeles, would be wide open for them. Their numbers were estimated to be in the hundreds of thousands.

There weren't more than five-hundred of us in the Castle.

I helped a truck full of soldiers offload their wounded. The outside of the truck was bloody. The soldiers looked pale and shrunken. Many of them were shaking.

"What's SF like?" I asked a girl as we offloaded a screaming man onto a stretcher.

"It's a living graveyard. They're everywhere."

"Do you know the woman everyone calls the Lady?" I asked her as she tried to walk away.

"Not really. I… our team hasn't been in contact with the main body for days. It wasn't part of the plan."

"Do you know…?"

"Listen, I've got work to do."

When we were finished getting the wounded onto helicopters coming from out of the south, the last of the Army came through the gap. There was even a tank. Seconds later, the bulldozer gassed its engine, belched black smoke, and moved to seal the entrance, and us, inside a "castle" that was about to be surrounded by hundreds of thousands of living corpses.

By dawn, guns were being handed out.

We were expecting the dead within two hours.

Just after eight o'clock, the first of them appeared on the horizon. I was on the right flank, below the wall. The overpass, where the main body of soldiers lay in wait with their guns, was above me and off to my left.

One of the soldiers was teaching us how to identify the different guns and ordinances we were supposed to use, and how to find and run ammo up onto the overpass when someone called for it.

The dead came on silently in twos and threes, sometimes alone, almost falling forward in the golden light of morning. Then they saw us and their voices rose into a howl of white noise.

Behind the leading corpses, a gray patchwork mass stretched off into the distance.

Snipers began to take out the stragglers, and quickly the call for "Three-Oh-Eight" rounds came down from the overpass into our little supply depot. Petersen, the soldier in charge of us, handed Ramos a case of ammo and sent him onto the overpass.

"Come back once you've dropped it," he ordered.

Above us, along the overpass, the gunfire was increasing. Now assault rifles were engaging closing targets.

"That'd be the three-hundred meter mark," muttered Petersen. "It's gonna get a lot closer than that. They'll start wanting Five-Five-Six, shortly." He handed me and Karen a crate. "Both of you carry this up when you hear 'em call out 'FIVE-FIVE-SIX'. Got it?"

We did.

The tank opened up from the other side of the overpass with a roar and a distant crack.

"We don't have any extra ammo for that one," laughed Petersen above the echo of its blast.

Now the heavy machineguns began to chatter away in the cold morning air.

"They're callin' for it! Go!" said Petersen, tapping us on the shoulders.

High up on the overpass, a man waved to us.

We lumbered awkwardly up the dirt berm and onto the old road that straddled the highway.

"Hurry! Hurry!" yelled the Waving Man.

All along the line, men and women swore amidst blue smoke and flying brass. The ground was littered with spent shells.

The tank roared again and the overpass shook.

I turned to see what the tank was firing at and saw a plume of dirt and smoke in the highway median far down the road. A sea of dead people surged forward, moved around the explosion, flew into the air above it and kept crawling forward through it. They covered every inch of the ground all the way to the far hills. They were fording a small river, crashing into the muddy brown water, crawling through the muck, heaving themselves up onto the banks. They lay in piles near the wall beneath the overpass, but still they came forward in long trains climbing atop the piles, gnashing their teeth, clawing their way toward the top of the overpass.

A kid with a shotgun ran down the line, stopping only to pump rounds and curse into the mindless faces below.

"Hurry!" I heard Karen say.

It wasn't just a nameless mass. It was a sea of dead people. Infected. Zombies.

I saw a man down there amongst them. He reminded me of one of my father's wealthy friends. He had the same chin. His eyes were wild, his skin gray, his gnashing teeth broken.

I saw children. Or once they had been children.

I saw a woman, beautiful before. She was running across the field below us. Even as an infected she still had grace. She must have been a runner once. The muscle memory still working af-ter... A bullet caught her in the head and sent her tumbling.

Heavy machineguns ripped through clusters of people where, for a fleeting moment, I thought I had seen some familiar face, as if there were only so many facial types in the world, and in every face was someone you had once known.

Sherry Taylor, my first kiss.

Watson Hughes, a kid who broke his arm one summer. We'd been best friends before the broken arm. But that summer separated us. I spent the summer at camp, fishing and hiking. When I returned, tanned and alive, we weren't the same anymore. We'd each found new friends.

Our path in the woods had diverged.

And...

It had made all the difference.

My brother Carter. That same shock of curly hair.

Others. So many others. Seeing all of them in the faces that came streaming across the dry brown fields of stubble and the muddy river, roaring for our blood and flesh, only to be blown to bits, cut in half, or horribly maimed right in front of our eyes.

They came on and on, and behind them seemed to be all the people that the world could hold. Except that they were no longer people.

"RPGs," yelled the Waving Man. "Get back down there and get us some more RPGs!"

I ran. I didn't know where Karen was. I passed Ramos sweating and smiling at me as he struggled under the weight of machine gun belts.

He said something.

The roar of gunfire was too loud. I leaned forward.

"I said," he said, "I wouldn't want to be the guy who fills out the forms for Reconstruction after this fight, Homes!" He laughed sharply in my ear.

"That guy up there wants RPGs," I told Petersen.

"People in hell want ice water!" Then, "Here, ya get two. That's all for now."

With one in each hand, I raced back up onto the overpass. My legs felt weak and tired. There was so much acrid blue gun smoke, I could hardly breathe.

"Hurry!" yelled the Waving Man.

I struggled along the firing line as hot brass shells landed on my arms, stinging and burning all at once. I couldn't protect myself from their hot touch because of the RPG in each hand.

Below and out there in the Sea of the Dead, Jordan Hastings, Natalie Wuhl, Farnsworth Bascomb, Sharon Chen, Uncle Bob, Ted Kennedy, Ronald Reagan, Mick Jagger. I felt I could see all of them in the masses that rolled forward, crushing and crashing into and through anything that stood between them and us.

Trees were falling.

Buildings were falling.

"Use those on that bridge!" the Waving Man shouted at me. "We need to slow 'em down. They're coming across the bridge too fast."

The kid with the shotgun inserted himself between us, pumped a round into the chamber, leaned over the side, and fired down into the crawling mass below.

"Take that ya bunch of freaks!"

Then he was down the line, cursing above the blare of gunfire.

"I don't know how to fire these things," I told the Waving Man.

He turned away from me, yelling toward someone down the line.

"I don't have time for this, son! We've got to take out that bridge ASAP."

"THEY'RE TUNNELING THROUGH THE GAP!" someone screamed below us.

"Aw hell!" said the Waving Man as he pointed at one of my RPGs. "Deploy this, snap that back, and fire. Simple. Now aim it and blow that bridge to hell."

The Waving Man ran off down the line.

I pointed the RPG at the bridge beyond the walls, farther down the highway. They were coming across it. Falling, shambling, racing. All of them.

I pressed the trigger, not expecting the thing to actually fire. The rocket raced away, twirling smoke, and impaled itself into the center of the bridge. Steel and metal and once-people arched away in a bright plume of flame.

I grabbed the other RPG.

I deployed. I snapped. I fired.

I aimed for the supports on the far side of the bridge.

The round would probably drop. I aimed higher.

I fired.

The rocket snaked away.

The bridge collapsed on one side, spilling the already horrified dead into the water.

I expected their faces to be indignant. As though it were a home video of a wedding on a pontoon boat suddenly giving way, spilling people into the water, ruining this grand event. But they surged mindlessly forward into the muddy current. The ones at the bank fell forward as those behind them trampled onward, piling up, piling upon a pile of... people.

Behind us, on the floor of the castle, flamethrowers were being used on the dirt berm that filled in the overpass. Holes were appearing as the living dead crawled out, covered in dirt. Soldiers raced back and forth spreading hot jets of flame as gray heads and scabby fingers pushed through the earth.

I ran back to Petersen.

"We ain't got much left and everybody wants something. Start grabbing everything and hauling it up there," he yelled in my ear above the mix of gunfire and the stadium roar of torment and hate that the dead made all around us beyond the earthen walls.

I grabbed an RPG and a crate of ammo and dragged them once more onto the overpass.

I could smell the gasoline from the flamethrowers above the blue smoke.

I heard the thick WHUMP WHUMP WHUMP of helicopter blades. Gunships came in low over the top of the overpass, guns burping out shadowy sprays of black lead into the crowd below.

The soldiers cheered, and still the Dead came on, gaping holes in their chests, missing arms, torn in half.

"What do I fire this at?" I said, holding up the RPG.

The Shotgun Kid looked at me as though I were stupid.

"Into them, ya moron!"

The dead were crawling upward, almost reaching the top of the berm.

"Anyone got shotgun rounds?" I heard the Kid ask.

I fired the RPG.

I didn't even aim. I just shot it into a moaning crowd approaching the base of the dirt wall below. A moment later, all the damage I'd done was washed away by another wave of scrambling corpses.

"Get back, you..." The Kid was swinging the shotgun down

onto the head of one of the dead who'd crawled up onto the overpass.

"Man down!"

To my right, a female soldier was being pulled over the heavy machinegun she was firing by a raving gray-fleshed man who had probably once been a construction worker before becoming a corpse. Another soldier that'd been feeding ammo into the gun backed away in horror as the dead suddenly surged forward around the woman machine-gunner.

I didn't think.

I know why now.

I had been here before.

Kathy Henderson-Kiel.

I launched myself forward. I grabbed the woman machine-gunner as I should have grabbed Kathy Henderson-Kiel as she was being pulled through the copy room wall.

As we tried to get up to the floor above.

As the dead beat on the flimsy door and came through the thin copy room walls.

Just after my fourth shame.

Everybody was dead. Derek. Carmichael. The people in the other buildings. Everyone. It was just the two of us now. On that floor alone.

Me and Kathy Henderson-Kiel.

The last woman I'd held as a woman… and made love to… and didn't love.

Could anything else but that have happened?

It happened.

I'm sorry Alex.

I needed you to be dead, because in my heart, you already were.

How could anyone survive what I'd seen on the streets below the Tower and in the shadowy stairwells all around me?

How could you still be alive, Alex?

My fourth shame is not that I made love to Kathy Henderson-Kiel in the copy room, but that I believed you were dead, Alex.

I gave up on you when I shouldn't have.

The woman gunner was going. Hauled over the top of the hot gun barrel. Disappearing into a gray forest tangle of scabby arms and teeth and dead-eyed lunatic faces.

I reached down into the dogpile of arms and leering grins and broken teeth, ignoring their raving groans and papery growls.

I found her legs and hauled her backward, both of us falling back onto the overpass.

The Shotgun Kid came in, pumping rounds and firing point-blank into the cluster that had tried to take her. They disintegrated in fleshy gray sprays under the withering blast of the shotgun.

"Get back on that gun!" yelled the Shotgun Kid.

The woman looked at her arms in horror.

"Am I bleeding?" she shrieked.

The other soldier, her assistant who had backed away, bent down. He was frantically looking for bite marks.

"Get back on that gun, mister!" whined the Shotgun Kid as he swung his weapon at a one-armed zombie crawling its way back up and over the guard rail.

The line. The thin line that had to be held.

I stumbled forward to the gun.

I rotated the barrel onto the crowd piling up just feet below, climbing up onto the bodies of the fallen, their fangs and eyes filled with all the malice the world had to offer.

"Pull the handle back on the side!" screamed the woman on the ground as she looked up at me with horror.

I pulled.

My hand was squeezing the trigger.

The gun roared to life and before I knew it, a belt of ammo was gone.

I felt electric.

I felt alive.

The woman crawled forward. She linked another belt and fed it into the gun.

"Keep going," she said, her voice trembling uncontrollably.

"Are you okay?" I asked.

"Fire!" she screamed through her tears.

I fired again, feeling the machinegun spit back its cold hatred into the faces of the clustering dead. I heard the woman sobbing as she linked another belt to the one that was threading its way into the machinegun.

Out on the horizon above the dead, a large plane with long swept-back wings and a thin body, its engines trailing black contrails, turned slowly off toward our left flank.

"What's that?" I asked over the roar of the powerful machinegun.

The woman kept sobbing. "Oh no," she mumbled as she looked up through tear-soaked eyes and saw the plane.

Below us, the finally dead were indistinguishable from the undead. Everything was a body. And through every body crawled eyes and teeth and claws. There were too many of them. Far too many of them.

"Airstrike inbound!" yelled the Waving Man as he ran down the line atop the overpass. "Get off the wall now! We're calling it in, Danger Close."

The Waving Man pulled people backwards, flinging them down onto the dirt berm inside the Castle. Other soldiers were leaping down themselves into the still-burning flames from the bodies of the zombies that had crawled through the dirt beneath the overpass.

"Get off the wall!" screamed the Waving Man.

"Get out of here!" I said to the sobbing woman as a wave of undead rose up in front of the barrel of the gun.

She wouldn't move.

I couldn't stop firing. The zombies were surging forward too quickly. I was sending short bursts at them whenever and wherever I saw movement.

We were the only ones left on the wall.

"Get off the wall now!" screamed the Waving Man, dragging the sobbing woman backward.

Off to our left, the bomber, a B-52 I think, leveled out. It would cross in front of the overpass in just seconds. I could see the pilots craning forward in their seats to see the ground below.

"Move!" yelled the Waving Man.

I kept firing. Out of the corner of my eye, I could see the bomb bay doors open on the plane.

Everything was so clear. And so real.

I left the gun and grabbed the other arm of the woman as the Waving Man dragged her toward the other side of the thin road atop the overpass.

The engines of the bomber quickly rose to a high-pitched whine that seemed to fill the entire world. All at once, they screamed as if the pilot were adding sudden and terrible power.

Zombies surged onto the roadway of the overpass directly behind us as we stumbled down the other side of the dirt wall and into the castle. Soldiers were firing at us. Firing at the zombies right behind us.

The jet streaked by as if going from slow motion to fast forward all at once.

I felt a hot wave of fire push us down off the hill, flinging us onto our faces into the burning, soft dirt.

It was over.

There weren't any more coming over the top of the hill. A few, on fire, crawled across the road and started down the other side as snipers finished them off.

Plumes of black smoke rose from beyond the overpass castle in the killing fields of the dead.

We crawled back to the top of the overpass.

On the other side, we saw the end of the world again.

Everything was on fire.

And still they flung themselves through it, only to burn and fall, and finally collapse, until there weren't any more of them left.

Everything smelled of gasoline.

The bomber was high in the sky, turning out toward the west, climbing away from our hell. Pillars of black smoke rose in anger as soldiers, all of us now, gathered ourselves from the ground.

The deafening roar of the engines and the blast of the bombs still rang in our ears, creating a soft silence that seemed to make the day unreal.

The Waving Man was back atop the overpass, binoculars held up, scanning the horizon.

"We beat 'em!"

Everyone cheered. They were glad to be alive. At least for one more day.

The gunner was peeling of her fatigues, looking for bite marks, her hands trembling. Her partner helped her.

"I'm good," she said, looking up, tears in her eyes. "I'm good." The man hugged her and then I could not tell if they were weeping or laughing.

I heard him sob, repeating, "I thought I'd lost you" over and over.

I found Karen holding a cigarette, her face blackened from the smoke of the fires, her tiny frame fading, as if barely holding on to existence.

I wondered how much further she would go.

How much further would we all go?

And then I looked in her eyes.

I heard my dad. Something he used to say. A line from an old movie.

From Here to Eternity.

"And we will all go from here to eternity."

Amongst the burning and the dying and the dead, one tiny woman, refusing to fade.

"Karen, I want to find this woman everyone calls the Lady. How would I do that?"

She stretched and looked around.

Somewhere we both heard a gunshot and neither of us jumped.

"The Army seems centered around that tank of theirs. We might want to check with them."

We found an officer, map in hand, clearing a space on the hood of a sedan.

"Excuse me."

He looked at me, the sudden hatred of the overworked flashing.

"I'm looking for someone they call the Lady. I think I might know her from… before everything."

"That so," he flattened his map and studied it for a moment.

"Excuse me!" I'd had enough.

He held up a hand.

"I heard you. That's what I'm all about here, right now. Her group drew off some runners who were all over us when we came down out of the pass. They haven't made it back. They're still out there. Who the hell are you with?"

"Reconstruction."

"Well, get yer team and saddle up. We're gonna ride out to their last known position and try to find 'em. Reconstruction might be some help."

An hour later, Karen was at the wheel of our Humvee. Ramos and I rode in back. Guy rode up front with Karen. We followed three sport utility vehicles that had seen better days. They were filled with soldiers.

We drove to the other side of the berm and out onto the highway heading west.

Corpses were everywhere. Unmoving. Silent. Finally dead.

We forded the shallow river, corpses floating along its banks, caught amongst the deadfall and clumps of other corpses. On the far side of the river, the highway ran straight west and we followed it.

Corpses that hadn't been people for a long time were flung in every direction.

Arms akimbo.

Arms thrown over rotting faces.

Legs splayed.

Legs missing.

Mostly whole.

Some parts missing.

In half.

Dirty.

Wild-eyed.

Gray.

Green.

Clean.

Horrified.

The hill that led up to the Altamont Pass rose in the hazy distance. Destruction was evident and everywhere. From buildings to blades of grass, there was little that had not been touched. Few things remained upright. It was as if a tidal wave had washed across the land of the living, and all that remained were dead sea-creatures that had once been us.

We saw the other trail of vehicle tracks and bodies off to the left.

We saw where sometime earlier another giant wave had crested and roared off to the southeast following the tire tracks. We drove to the point of departure... where the attempt to draw off the infected had separated from the line of retreat.

The Point of Departure.

There is so much weight to those words. I realize now that words have weight. All words. All words carry a weight that must be shouldered through a lifetime of memory.

The Point of Departure.

Only at the end do I understand words now. Their meaning. Their weight. Their cost.

On the highway, a lone straggler stood as they sometimes do, staring up at the late morning sun. I could feel the hesitation we all felt.

Is it one of them?

Or just some lost survivor, fritzed out. Unable to take one more minute of sanity.

Point of Departure, also.

But as the convoy slows, the straggler lurches toward the lead vehicle. The movement is tired and in the moment it begins to turn toward us, we know. A moment later, I hear the blast and know the Shotgun Kid is riding in the lead vehicle.

He and Carmichael would get along.

I think of the stairwell.

Home run.

Guy, inspired by the indiscriminate termination of a single zombie without all the required tests, begins to rant about survivors they've found. Survivors who have lost it and begun to wander with the infected, covered in gore, dirty, but not infected. Just undetected by the corpses who must assume this survivor is merely one of them. It usually ends badly.

For a moment, I am tired. But then, as I write this, I remember thinking at that moment, I felt that Alex might be close. That I would find her. That if I could have just that...

...I remember thinking the world could have the rest.

That the zombies could tear us down, tear down our cities and our towns and our apartments in expensive buildings and drag our closest friends on earth down into a stairwell of arms and teeth or through a wall of gray limbs and hungry moans.

But if I could just have Alex...

If I could have Alex, the world could have the rest.

I'll take Alex. You keep Manhattan.

We turned left and followed the swath of damage. Their passage, the passage of the dead, had left a wide track, narrower than the main assault on the castle, but wide enough to show us their weight.

We passed the occasional corpse, a bullet in the head, or the head missing altogether.

I wonder how long they will rot out here in the fields under the sun. Out here, forever, and then I remember Reconstruction. My job. Why we, the Reconstruction team will come and Reconstruct.

I have come for something else, someone else.

And in my own way, Reconstruction also.

Ahead a little ways, we pass an overturned Land Rover. The driver, one of them now, is pinned beneath the wreck, just like that other wreck, the wreck of Ferrari Man from so many days ago that it feels like another life. He gnashes his teeth, his skin still clear, not turned corpse gray, or mottled or torn.

"This her vehicle?" asks the Shotgun Kid as he dismounts and points the shotgun lazily at the head of the pinned driver.

The driver gnashes his teeth, almost swearing gutturally.

Ka-boom.

Home run.

"She ain't in there," says the Kid.

I hear someone from inside the lead vehicle say something muffled about the trail and continuing on.

"Guy, make sure you note these bodies. We need to come back and do our job," instructs Karen.

"They must have gone on foot after the vehicle flipped," whispers Ramos. His voice is breathy and dry. "They can't be very far away."

The trail enters a dry brown cornfield, reminding us that it is beyond fall and that the harvest is late. The trail isn't so definite, but the violence done to it is intensified. There are more bodies, and I can hear Guy talking to himself as he hurries to write down the counts and locations.

"They'll be all over this field. So we'll have to be thorough." Karen again.

The vehicles push through the growth like we're on some third-world extreme expedition instead of a cornfield in central California. The dry brown stalks part and the vehicles gun their engines up onto a parking lot.

We halt in front of an old country school. The Army vehicles circle wide, signaling for us to stand by. For a moment, I see a dark shape behind a window and I want to believe I've seen short blond hair. That I have seen Alex.

I only want to see that.

The Army completes their sweep and the soldiers dismount, heavy rifles pointing toward the old schoolhouse door.

There are corpses lying on the steps, but the doors are shut.

The soldiers form into a wedge and begin their slow walk to the front steps.

I leave the vehicle then.

I think Karen was calling to me, telling me to get back inside.

I'm right behind the soldiers when they tear the doors off the hinges with some special tool. The jaws of life, ironically. In the dusty dark, a large, well-built, once-black man, a recently infected, lurches forward, the whites of his eyes rolling in his skull.

The Shotgun Kid fires and the man crumples back against the doorway.

The Kid enters with two soldiers in tow.

There are three blasts on the heels of automatic gunfire.

I run for the doors, but a soldier grabs me and drags me to the hot pavement.

The Kid comes out, smoke still rising from the mouth of his shotgun as he thumbs shells into the breach.

I think I was screaming. In my head I heard myself very calmly asking if she was in there. If Alex was okay. In my head I sounded very calm.

But I think I was screaming.

The kid, young, jaded, hard, tough, everything I wanted to be at the moment, walked by me. Then he turned back. There wasn't an ounce of compassion in his cold eyes.

"Not anymore, mister."

The world is cruel, and filled with Low Men.

Karen led me inside. I was sobbing. I was a wreck. I saw the body in the corner of the room. There were shell casings everywhere, bodies flung at various angles, hands and arms akimbo and away. As if refusing to believe that what has happened to them, has happened.

But all I could see was blond hair.

Blondie.

From that band back in the eighties.

And when they turned her over...

It wasn't Alex.

Even the hair was different. More like that singer Roxette. Not Blondie. A Different face. Angular and tough.

Only recently a zombie, and shortly thereafter, finally dead.

I screamed at the officer in charge, "Is that her? Is that the Lady?"

He seemed to look at the body for a long time. "Yeah," he whispered. "That was her."

But it wasn't Blondie.

It wasn't Alex.

I'm not crazy. It was not her.

Which means she could still be alive.

I had thought for a second I might be crazy. Karen checked Roxette's ID.

Amanda Something-or-other.

That was her name.

Not Alex Watt.

Which means…

Goodbye.

I'm leaving now. It's just after two o'clock in the morning. We're back at the AmeriCal gas station in Turleyville. I'm going to look for Alex.

I will find her.

Even if I have to search forever.

Even Roland must surely reach the top of the Dark Tower.

I never finished the last book in the series. I don't even know what it's called. The device I was listening to only contained the first six books.

But I knew, I know, Roland must reach the top of his Dark Tower.

And I…

I will find Alex.

I'm leaving this journal. I'm leaving most everything. I don't need it anymore.

I've come this far on my quest.

I'll take one thing.

Just as Roland took his guns, I'll take my compass.

My compass will lead me back to the woman I love.

I'll cover myself in corpse goo from the body pile behind the gas station. And then, like Roland pursing the Man in Black, I'm going to pursue Alex with my compass across this desert of zombies our country has become.

I can't wait for her to be added to the database by record or photograph. I can't wait for her to end up like all the dead in the kill zone at the foot of the castle. It'll be too late then.

I'll go and walk among them until I find her. I'll look in each face until I do.

I know my heart wants to find her, and I believe in love now.

That's what I've learned from this crossing of the United States. I've learned four things about love.

Four things about myself.

Four things about all of us.

One, I believe love can conquer death.

Looking at the woman in the schoolhouse who should have been Alex, but wasn't, I understand that a corpse, a funeral, the goodbye at the end of a long illness in the hospital, doesn't mean you stop loving someone. It means you love them even more. And, if there is even the hope that you might have one minute more with the one you love, then you will search through every zombie-infested city in this American wasteland for that minute. You will wait as the minutes pass and the pulse slows, and though life continues around the two of you in that hospital, you will hold onto every moment and be grateful afterward that you did. Then you will stand by an open grave until Low Men drag you from its side.

Two, I believe that love is enough.

After death takes everything, love remains. The machine gunner and her husband. What he'd said to her in that moment when he knew he wouldn't lose her to the infection. In those terrible moments as she searched for scratches and bites, she was dead, he knew it and she knew it.

And then she was okay.

And in his sobs of relief I heard love go on living, despite death's threat. Despite death's lie that it won't.

It does.

Three, I believe all those things about love that people sing about.

I've been thinking about songs. Songs since I saw the body in the schoolhouse. Songs about love.

I should have paid more attention to the words of all those songs. We all should have.

If you could sing, or even speak those words softly, right now, to the one you love... it wouldn't matter whether you could or couldn't sing. It wouldn't matter to them at all.

Trust me.

You could try Sam Cooke's Wonderful World.

Y'know, don't know much about all those subjects. But I do know that I love you. And I know that if you love me too, what a wonderful world this would be.

If there's someone you could say those words to right now... say them.

And Four, Love is bigger than we let it be. Bigger than we can imagine.

I came this far on love. Farther than at first I thought I would need to go. Just like Roland. When The Gunslinger began, I thought Roland would find his Man in Black on the other side of the desert. But it's gone so much further. Further than we expected it would.

And so have I.

I believe it doesn't matter what I did, or what Alex did, or what has become of us both. Dead. Undead. Surviving.

I believe in love now.

More now than when I first began to pursue Alex across this desert.

———————

I wish I had your faith, Jason. I hope you find her.

—Karen Haines, Incident Reconstruction Team Leader

Historical Artist's Note

There is no official record that indicates the dispositions of persons mentioned within this story as there is in the last account. That summary was prepared in the year that followed the Plague and discovered later within the archives of the Department of Reconstruction's Museum. Instead, I offer two documented historical summaries of two unique features mentioned within Jason Hamilton's account.

Major "Bebe" Firestein's legendary stories are recounted in several survivor accounts from the period. Though Jason Hamilton's account seems to be the end of Major Firestein, many accounts indicate that he and several soldiers escaped after being stranded by General Pettigrew.

Major "Bebe" Firestein was not actually an American army officer. He was the acting Israeli attaché to the Pentagon when the Plague first broke out. With air travel severely restricted, Major Firestein joined U.S. forces and took command of a small ad hoc commando unit that helped secure the Brooklyn Bridge, so a ragtag U.S. Army could finally begin operations to liberate Manhattan.

After joining the mission to reconnect the coasts and being stranded outside New Orleans, tales of Major Firestein's exploits become more like that of a mythical figure from the wild west. One report has him rescuing survivors from off the roof of a mall in Colorado. Another report tells of him perishing when the last holdouts of the Second Alamo constructed their own dirty bomb and set it off just as the fort was being overrun by an infected mob, estimated at upwards of thirty-thousand. The last report comes from Israel. One hundred years after the Plague, an elderly Rabbi released a deathbed account saying that Bebe Firestein had returned years ago to Israel, after twenty years abroad. He'd had many more adventures beyond what was reported, and for the last fifteen years of his life he'd worked as a cobbler near the Temple Mount.

The crew of the B-52 bomber mentioned in this account flew over one-hundred and three missions during the Plague. Most of us are aware of their story as told in the book and later the movie The Crew. On their legendary ninety-fifth mission, the crew of the stricken bomber unanimously agreed to go over their target a second time after a massive mechanical failure prevented the bomb bay doors from opening on the initial strike run. Down to just one engine, they returned to strike the target, The Embarcadero, near The Ferry Building in downtown San Francisco, where survivors had been holding out since the initial outbreak. Knowing they would have to fly at a dangerously low altitude and avoid several downtown buildings and the Bay Bridge to be able to strike the target effectively, all on emergency engine power and in a mechanically unstable aircraft, Captain Stacey McQueen asked the crew for a vote on whether to complete the mission to relieve the survivors trapped in the Ferry Building, with the realization that they would most likely not survive the attack run, or to attempt to return to base safely so the aircraft could be repaired.

The crew voted, unanimously, to complete its mission.

One hundred and seventy-two survivors were rescued that day, including future President of the United States of America, Matthew Hsu, who was only eight at the time. In a rare moment of cooperation, the New California Republic and the United States of America agreed to award all five crew members the Congressional Medal of Honor. Three years after the final mission, number one-hundred and three, eight missions beyond their most famous, Captain Stacey McQueen, co-pilot Lt. James Savola, Navigator Constantine Blum, Bombardier Wayne Smith, and Crew Chief SSG Jennifer Samuels received the nation's highest award for "completing their mission in the face of certain death." Crew Chief Samuels, the last survivor of the very long-lived group, was laid to rest with the words, "Mission Complete" engraved on her tombstone just as it had been with the rest of her fellow crewmembers. This account of Jason Hamilton witnessing a close air support strike by the most famous aircraft and crew of all time was a rare and unexpected gift for those of us who spend our days amongst the dusty stacks of history, keeping the flame of heroes-past burning, long after they have faded away.

Part Three: Redemption

Historical Artist's Note

There is so much that survives this period. And often, so little that didn't. We have only references to some materials, books, digital songs, and art that failed to survive the collapse of the world during the time of the Plague. Recently, Chu Hingston, a Hardrive Archeologist most notable for unlocking the secrets of the Gates Drive, uncovered a collection of music by an artist known as Bob Marley. Nothing is known about this long-lost musician other than a few books that endured the various conflagrations that broke out as survivors burned everything they could to keep the undead at bay, and to survive the cold nights of the winters that followed. Most survivors assumed the information contained within those blackening texts would survive somewhere else, or it simply did not matter to them at the time. The need for fuel to defend themselves, cook their meals, or survive bitterly cold nights seemed more pressing in the moment of those days.

The few texts that remain reference Bob Marley as having died long before the Plague. Chu Hingston shared with me some of the songs of Bob Marley he'd recovered. One in particular struck me profoundly and even stayed with me through the days and nights as I began to finish this project. Maybe its influence was too much. Maybe I am reading into these final accounts what I want to read. Maybe I just wished for something better for these two people. But that is the art form of the Historical Artist. We take the past and glue it together, looking for the connections that may never have been. There is no solid evidence that either of these personal accounts reference the other, or that their subjects are connected. I will repeat this. "There is no solid evidence that either of these personal accounts reference the other." This piece should never be mistaken for a historical account. There is no definite evidence that these accounts are one coherent story. In all likelihood, they are the statistically probable coincidences that must arise with a numerical population in excess of seven billion at the time of the Plague. The Alex and Jason of these accounts may not have known each other. Each may have had their own "Alex" and "Jason" in mind as they left their last handprint in the permanent record of a world changing into something new.

And yet, there is this...

Consider the unpublished works of Jonah Clement, Post-Plague Reporter for The Los Angeles Times. The story I have chosen to end this piece with was never filed. It was written toward the end of Mr. Clement's too-short career, and although records indicate the article was due to be published, it was in actuality, never published. The California Republic-Nevada States War broke out the day before the article was to run. Publication of the article was put on hold, as it was considered a "soft" piece. Mr. Clement was killed in action reporting from Las Vegas a few weeks later. The Times server, a pre-Plague operating system, was virtually destroyed in the air campaign of the following year. For several years, the damaged server was warehoused. Recently, a graduate student, Kevin Tolles, managed to salvage the hard drive for his master's thesis, and the documents contained within were summarily stored on a secure Museum of Reconstruction DECA-RAID Vault Server and given special public access.

I offer Mr. Clement's article for your final consideration...

LA Times, 23 May

File this under "Whatever became of?" You know you love it when we tell you what really happened to some celebrity during the Plague. Was the President really a zombie? Did that guy from the Star Trek go cannibal? Well, it's been fifteen years of my infamous "Whatever became of?" pieces. Today I'd like to share with you my own personal "Whatever became of?"

It's not about a famous person. But it is about a hero. A man who rescued me from certain death back when things were looking pretty dark for all of us. One of the first pieces I wrote for The Times was an account of how I was rescued. As many of you know, I was trapped in Lake Tahoe when the Plague broke out. I spent eight weeks on an island in the middle of Lake Tahoe with some other survivors, making raids into South and North Shore for supplies. We weren't very good, and we kept losing people on each raid. In the end, it was just me. A lot of you know how I felt right about then. I was alone, frightened, and very tired. I felt like giving up. I didn't think it was ever going to get any better. You probably had a similar experience if you lived through that time. In fact, if you're alive, you've probably felt that way at one time or another. Long story short, I was rescued by a guy named Cal Stevens. He was a ranger for the California Parks Department. He was much older than me. He was tall and wiry, lean and hard, a real man from the yesterdays of long ago. The things I remember most about him are his arctic blue eyes and gray hair, shaved over the neck and ears.

He was a good man.

With all the rhetoric heating up between L.A. and Vegas these days, I thought it might be good to check back in with Cal. He's kind of a compass for me. It might be time for us to remember what good men, and good people, were really like.

Cal died this morning.

The nursing home where he'd been living for the last five years, called me a few hours ago. I was his last visitor. I visited him a week ago Tuesday, and I was still working on this piece when I got the call about the man who'd saved my life. For some backstory, here is what I wrote about Cal back then. It was my first piece with the LA Times.

The gas needle has fallen to empty, but the ranger knows we have a few more miles left in the tank. The last three gas stations have been too dangerous to stop at. Too many zombies are wandering the streets with dusk coming on.

We drive through the late fall evening and I look over at the Ranger, seeing his face in the panel lights. His faded blue eyes are watching the highway ahead.

We are passing through farm country that runs the length of the Central Valley along the Ninety-Nine corridor.

I wonder if it seems unchanged to Ranger Stevens, no different tonight than all the years of his long life. The fields have grown wild. The harvest had risen and lain all through those last hot days of summer and into fall. Now as we pass these roads in the night, hunting for a gas station, the fields look tangled, unkempt, and full of death to me.

We have been listening, quietly, to old-school country music. Marty Robbins, Johnny Cash, and even the occasional Johnny Horton. We're listening to a tape, playing from an actual tape deck in Cal's old pickup truck. Imagine that.

Ahead, we approach a Decontamination Command Convoy. Big armored trucks lie idling in plumes of exhaust alongside the highway in the grass next to the off-ramp.

"We're buttoning up for the night," says the watch sergeant when the ranger pulls his old Ford alongside the platoon that will guard the trucks for the night. They seem to know each other from times past when the ranger has come in to report.

"I think I might drive on to L.A. tonight. Found this kid up on the Lake and they're gonna want a report before they send you boys up there," says Cal.

"Got coffee?" asks the watch sergeant.

"Some. Need gas more."

"We cleared a station a few miles south of here, one-horse town. Looks like they made a good show of it. We topped off from their pumps and left the power running. Might try there."

"Thanks. S'pose I will," says Ranger Stevens.

He reaches forward to shift the truck into gear, and for a moment the sergeant backs away. Then he steps forward again.

"Bad up there on the Lake, Cal?"

The ranger stares forward.

He was old before all this started. Long, lean, rangy, he'd worked ranches and livestock for most of his sixty-five years. His hair is gray and cropped, his skin tanned by sun and wind. For all his years, he doesn't seem so old. Until you look into his eyes. It's the eyes that make him old. Older than anyone could ever possibly imagine.

"Bad enough," answers Ranger Stevens.

The sergeant backs away and we drive off into the night.

A few miles down the road, we circle the little gas station town that once thrived alongside the highway. There is the gas station, one of those mart and multi-pump food court types. A fast food restaurant sits long abandoned on the other side of the road, a burnt-out vehicle in the intersection that separates them. Farther down, away from the highway, there is an old garage. In the midnight gloom, it looks a source of trouble.

Corpses litter the street. They are finally dead now.

After the ranger is sure there aren't any stragglers about, he pulls up next to the pumps. He turns off the vehicle and we wait.

If there are any, they'll come for us now.

They will be mere cutout figures, people-shaped monsters of nothingness in the foreground of night.

We sit listening to the small ticks of the old truck and the quiet in-between them. Cal wonders in a whisper, when he might ever hear a bird again. He ruminates that on a night like this, he should have at least heard an owl or a bat.

We leave the truck and Cal takes his 30.06 hunting rifle with him. He always wears the Colt Forty-Five revolver strapped to his hip. He has since August.

The Decon team has left the bodies piled in front of the barricade, against the doors and boarded up windows of the gas station. We see the dried blood and dark gore.

Cal steps gingerly, as though tracking a deer across a forest floor, through and around the pile of bodies.

Inside, Cal gets the pumps started.

"They'd held for a while at least," he says as he inserts the pump nozzle into the tank back at the truck.

I look at where the zombies had gotten into the gas station.

Near the bathrooms, a back door has been forced off its hinges. It must have been a real fight.

I watch Ranger Stevens study the town.

The restaurant across the way looks like a hollowed out corpse.

The burnt vehicle.

The gas station where someone, or a bunch of someones, had made their last stand.

I almost hear the ranger's thoughts. He's wondering about the survivors, if they're out there somewhere. Are they infected now, wandering cold fields in the pale blue moonlight? Or are they all lying in front of other gas stations? Or are they alive, still running for their lives out in the wilderness?

Above the building, a sign reads AmeriCal Gas. Another sign welcomes us to Turleyville.

When the tank is full, Ranger Stevens replaces the nozzle, climbs back into the truck, and we sit for a while. It will be a long haul to Los Angeles tonight. He tells me he is getting old and doesn't sleep as well as he used to. He pulls out his paperwork and maps, and notes Turleyville for "Reconstruction".

"They can decide what to do with it back in L.A.," he adds as an epitaph.

He starts the old truck and the cassette again. We ease back onto the highway. We are just red tail lights on a dark night. We are alive."

So, that's a piece I wrote fifteen years ago. Here's what I was working on after my meeting with Cal last week.

Cal Stevens retired from the Ranger Service about six years back. Five years ago, he moved into the Verde Pines retirement community. For the last year, he's been living in the assisted wing.

He's got some memory problems, not full-blown Alzheimer's, no one has that anymore, but let's just say the past is very real to him. He gets very emotional. Cal is thin, gray, almost shrunken. Only in the eyes do I see the man that rescued me all those years ago. Sometimes.

I ask Cal what he remembers most about the Plague.

He has his own story of survival.

He's a man who was raised from birth to know how to live off the land. He spent the worst six weeks of the Plague deep in the Sierra Nevadas before he started finding other survivors. He was a quiet man back then. The week we spent together, driving down through the zombie-infested remains of Northern California and into the Reclamation Zone, held very few conversations. In fact, I cannot remember a single conversation in detail.

I do remember feeling safe around him.

I tell him that.

His eyes begin to moisten. I realize I have not heeded the nurse's warning.

"Mistah Cal," as she calls him, "is very sensitive now. So don't poke around in the past too much. It's hard on him, child." She really calls me "child".

I'm glad Cal Stevens has her to take care of him. Still, I've gone too far. He tells me it's good to have me there with him. He tells me he's never missed an article I've written. He often used his vacations to catch up on the pieces he'd missed while working in the deep woods.

He tells me about the years after the Plague he'd spent working in the forests. In those simple bedside conversations, we stumble onto something amazing. It's a small thing, but it amazes me nonetheless.

Cal terminated the last recorded Plague zombie.

For the last ten years of Cal's career with the Ranger Service, he worked as a sort of animal control officer. Once the big cities were cleared and most of the Iinfected were gone, there were relatively few attacks. But every now and then he'd get a call, usually out in the hinterland, and he'd have to go out and "clean up the remains". His words.

"I took care of the last one, oh, about two years before I retired," he tells me from his bed.

It's official and I can look it up if I choose to. I did, and it is.

I ask him to tell me about the last zombie to walk the earth.

He watches the window and the garden beyond for a moment. He begins to speak without looking at me, like he's back on that day.

"I got a call from local law enforcement that they'd seen a zombie up around Pinecrest Lake, near a little town called Strawberry. We really hadn't had any sightings that year and it was already well into fall. We didn't get too many calls in winter as they tended to freeze up. Stay put. Summer was the worst back in those first years after. You'd get a bite, kids playing out in the woods. That was bad. But as the years passed, the ones we found weren't doing so good. I guess all those years were pretty hard on 'em.

"That entire summer, we hadn't received one call. I think there was even money down that we might go the whole year without getting called out to put at least one down. But in the end, just toward the last of the good weather, you could tell it was the last of the good days before things got real cold, that was when I got the call.

"I'd planned to do something else that weekend. I always got a haircut on Friday afternoon. The barbershop where I went, had a beautiful painting of the Sierra Nevada Mountains. Two deer in a meadow. I loved that painting. I know those places inside those pictures. I've been there.

"So I got my deer rifle, loaded up the truck, and drove on up toward Sonora, which never really recovered from the Plague, then on into the mountains. It was a beautiful day. I remember it now like it was yesterday. The sky was so blue. So startlingly blue. The sun at that altitude felt good and warm coming through the windshield of my old truck.

"I pulled up to a general store in Strawberry, which was all there really was of that town. The only other building was a cabin rental place across the road. It was mostly quiet up there in summer. Winter skiing was the thing. I could hear the sound of the wind moving through the pines. I could hear the distant roar of the river nearby.

"I talked to a fellow in the store. He told me the reports were coming from some cabin owners over near the south ridge. He showed me where on the map and I took the truck over.

"I'll say this about time. At that moment, I wouldn't have picked that day out of ten-thousand. But here, now, lying in this bed coughing, I'd give anything for just one more day like that day. To be out in the woods. I could smell the heavy dust of a long, dry summer when I parked the truck. All that summer dust, thick and heavy and almost sweetened by the pines. Winter would come soon and wash all of it away.

"It was quiet. Sound traveled that afternoon almost like it was a clear thing all to itself. Even now, lying in this bed, I can hear the sound my old door made on that truck. How it whined for just a second when I opened it. The metallic clang when it closed. I must have heard that sound more times than can be counted, or should be for that matter. But right here, now, I can hear it plain as day and it's like the voice of a friend I haven't heard from in some time.

"I took my rifle and walked down the mountain. They almost always move downwards, it's easier for them. There was a river down there and I knew the zombie would be near it. The noise of it attracts 'em.

"I passed cabins that had been closed up for the summer. Like I said, it's mostly ski cabins up there because of the big slopes farther up the mountain.

"But they like to get in and around those cabins. Look for a dog, or a child.

"I checked each of the cabins to make sure it hadn't gotten into one. That might make a nasty surprise for some skiers showing up late one night. Most of the Plague zombies are now so decrepit and falling apart that people can just dodge by 'em. But if they get the jump on you, it can be a little tricky.

"I picked up some signs near a cabin at the bottom of the hill, scratch marks on the front door. I found the drag marks. One leg pulling a dragging foot, and after that it wasn't too long until I found him. Straight line down to the river. I saw him far of. Upstream behind some boulders.

"I maneuvered close enough along the big river rocks so I could get a better shot at him. I didn't want him slipping into the river. Then I'd have to issue a quarantine alert. So I thought I'd get up on one of the big rocks and try to knock him back away from the river when I took the shot.

"In the process of doing that, I dropped my rifle. It clattered against a rock and almost went skittering off into the water, but I caught it up just 'fore it did. Woulda been a tragedy. I took a deer every year with that gun. My nephew has it now. Good boy. Ranger service too. I like that he carries my old rifle. They wouldn't let me have it in here now."

Silence.

"When I got my rifle up and sighted, I expected him to be scrambling over the rocks to get at me because of the noise my rifle had made. But he didn't. He was mad, for sure, hissing at me and all. But he hadn't moved.

"Then I saw the hand come up into my scope, just under the crosshairs.

"I had to check my scope, make sure there wasn't something on it. When I sighted in again, sure enough, she was clutching at him. Holding onto him. There were two of 'em.

"She was torn in half. Years ago probably. But she'd dragged herself along all these years. Here she was now, holding onto him. He was falling apart, hair in scraps, skin in shreds, white bone, long exposed in places. Standard long-term infection.

"I knew I had a plan when I took the first shot. I can't remember exactly what it was, but I had a plan. I think I thought that if I shot the female first, he'd come after me. He'd leave her and start out across the rocks for me. I could take him once I was sure he wouldn't get into the river and contaminate it.

"My first shot put her down. It went right into her skull and she didn't move after that."

Silence.

Cal wipes at a tear in eyes I have watched fill with memories.

"Her hand let go of him then. I could hear my shot echoing off the far rim as I snapped the bolt back, ejected the spent shell, and put the bolt forward with a new round. It was that kind of day when everything is so clear… and sky blue and… golden. The deep shade of the forest and the sound of the river is all around me. And I knew summer was over then."

Silence. Cal's eyes are watering. His mouth twitches as he chews at a convulsion within.

"It's okay Cal," I tell him. "We can stop now."

He continues to chew. He's crying when he looks up at me.

The nurse comes in.

I'm in trouble.

"Mistah Cal, what you all upset about now, honey?" she asks, as though we are boys behaving badly and one of us has hurt the other.

"He loved her. He wouldn't leave her," sobs Cal.

The nurse sits on the bed and holds Cal to her chest. This once strong ranger, frail, now more a child, an infant, sobs into her and she murmurs words of comfort.

I am going.

I am at the door.

I am unclean and cause misery.

"He wouldn't leave her," bellows Cal through wet runny tears. "He kept right by her side, hissing and raging at me. But he would not leave her."

Through the tears, I hear this once strong, silent man begin to ask if the unknown can be known.

"I never seen anything like that in all my years of a world I learned long ago I would never understand. But he wouldn't leave her. He just stood there… waiting for me to shoot him." And Cal begins to cry even harder. And I realize I am not brave enough to hear his tears. Their ache is soul deep.

I am going.

I am at the door.

I am unclean and cause misery.

"Let me finish," wails the frail old man who is still my hero. "Please let me finish and be done with this forever."

"No, Mistah Cal, everything gonna be alright," comforts the nurse. "We put those things away for now."

"No, come back here, boy!" And the iron of the ranger I once knew is back. The ranger who pulled me off that drifting boat that would have, in time, come to rest on the zombie-infested beaches of the North Shore Casinos.

"What Cal? What is it you want to tell me?"

For a moment he is lost. He cannot remember what it was he was going to say, as though the sudden appearance of who he is now has distracted him.

"What happened next?" I prompt. "By the river that day. That last day of summer."

Then Cal remembers.

"Can they love each other? Do you know that, boy? Do you know if they can do that?"

I didn't have an answer. Who could?

He stops there, as if to make sure I'm following him. But that isn't it. That's not the end.

"I pulled the trigger and he went down," wails Cal into the nurse.

And as he sobs into her chest, this is what I hear.

"The last one was the worst. He loved her. All those zombies, all those years, they'd become nothing more than animals, less than even, and the last of them turned on me in the end. I was glad they were the last. He loved her. He wouldn't leave her," he sobs over and over into his nurse.

"No, Mistah Cal…" she murmurs. "No, honey…"

When I read the official report, I learn that Cal went back to his truck, filled out the paperwork, and got a camera and a can of gasoline.

The last two zombies had no identification. Just some personal effects. The yellowing paper of the official report reads:

Female, one diamond ring, left ring finger.

Male, one battered army compass, worn around the neck.

The nurse glares at me until I leave. As I go, I can her singing.

"Everything's gonna be alright."

I hear Cal crying.

In the hall, I wait until he stops. I need that. I need to know that he will forget, and that sometimes, forgetting is not such a curse.

But I will not forget them.

I will remember, even if I did not know who they were.

Historical Artist's Note

"Redemption Song", by Bob Marley.

About the Author

Nick Cole is a former soldier and working actor living in Southern California. When he is not auditioning for commercials, going out for sitcoms or being shot, kicked, stabbed or beaten by the students of various film schools for their projects, he can be found writing books. He's the author of *The Old Man and the Wasteland*, *CTRL ALT REVOLT!*, and *Soda Pop Soldier* among others. Check out all his books at nickcolebooks.com

CPSIA information can be obtained
at www.ICGtesting.com
Printed in the USA
FSOW03n1511111116
27208FS